MEMOIRS OF A

CRAZY

Memoirs of a Crazy

A novel by Charles M.

www.charlesmbooks.com

ISBN 978-0-9985391-0-2
1st Edition

Deep Anchor Publishing
707.492.5755
www.deepanchorpublishing.com

For Elizabeth, Carter, Penny, and Charlie

March 22, 1967

It's just barely turned spring, but it still feels like full on winter up here. It's been snowing just a little bit each night. In the morning, it's hard and frozen, and by the afternoon it's a bit mushy. Confuses the senses and makes it hard to keep the house clean. I guess being this far north has its advantages and its disadvantages as well. I've spent the last few days chopping the wood I cut down last year. When you give it a year to dry out, it splits like it's not even there. I love doing it this time of year when the air is crisp and fresh, and the sun struggles to gain relevance. I had a peculiar feeling a few days ago. I find myself sometimes being overtaken by the way the ax moves through the wood. It's so...perfect. Including the sound. It's crisp. I heard a similar sound when splitting open a head of lettuce a few days ago. The feeling is strange but somehow soothing. I can't really explain it. Maybe this is why I have a massive pile of wood behind my house. I took a small truckload over to Mrs. Denison last week. She's getting so old. I can't help but think the next time I see her will be the last. She repeats herself a lot. Constantly asking me the same questions over and over. Bruises all over her skin. I'm afraid she might be losing her mind. Somehow, she still manages to take care of herself. Poor Mrs. Denison. A widow of many years now, I'm not sure she even has any family left to take care of her. With her mind slipping, it's only a matter of time before they find her frozen out on the lake with no clothes. I feel so bad that she can't do very many things anymore. A tiny part of me wants to put her out of her misery.

Our country is in turmoil right now. I'm not sure where the world is headed anymore. Now it seems we're getting involved in Vietnam. A war we don't belong in. So much hatred. So much violence. It confuses me sometimes. It stirs this thirst...I can't describe it. It's a hunger...a lust that never goes away. I push it out of my head, but it always comes back. I find myself behind the house with my eyes closed and my head shaking back and forth. It's a madness...like Mrs. Denison? I feel like I'm changing. I feel I'm about to find my true calling. I used to think I wasn't needed in this world. I used to think I didn't belong. But now, more than ever, when splitting wood, I've realized it needs me. Mrs. Denison needs me. I've had thoughts come in mind...evil thoughts. I want to help people. I want to help the world. I feel like I can hear them calling me to help. Begging me to help them. Not their regular voice, but their inner voice. They talk to me often, and they talk loud. They always ask me the same thing. Every. Single. Time. They ask me to set them free...

—Patrick

March 27, 1967

I can't ignore the calls and cries anymore. The more I try to block them out, the louder they get.

Insisting I help them. Insisting that I'm the only one that can do it. It's as if they trust me. And I take this responsibility seriously. Poor Mrs. Denison has been begging me as of late, and the screams for sweet mercy keep getting louder. We found her in her bathroom this morning. She looked to be in bad shape. Poor Arthur couldn't stomach looking at her, so I had to do most of the heavy lifting. Arthur just doesn't see things the way they are. The natural order of things. Yes, Mrs. Denison is an old lady, with wrinkly skin and sagging body parts, but that's what happens when you get old. It's going to happen to everyone who gets to that age. I just stay strong knowing there will always be people like me to support them and give them what they want. I feel like a lion...an up and coming lion that is just finding its territory. The hunger for blood is primal. I believe it's an ancient calling from long ago. The desire to kill...I don't have time to think of that because right now I'm king of the safari.

We finally managed to get Mrs. Denison into her bed and comfortable. I directed Arthur to go into the kitchen and cook her an acceptable breakfast while I sat and had a conversation with her. The kinds of conversations that Arthur didn't understand. Only me. While Arthur cracked eggs and sizzled the bacon, I went into a deep conversation with Mrs. Denison. Let me remind you that it wasn't her physical voice that talked to me, but her soul. Mrs. Denison is really a swell old lady. She told me of her late husband, Samuel. She spoke with the wonder of a young woman in love. As I watched her lips moving, I had to remind myself that I was sitting in front of a demented, old lady. Mrs. Denison told me how Samuel swept her off her feet. They eloped together when she was only sixteen years old. They didn't have a care in the world. We laughed some as she talked about how good looking she used to be. She even joked about losing her mind. That's when the conversation got serious. She pleaded with me to make it go away. I was hesitant at first, but when you are really talking to the soul and not just the body of someone, it's not really words but more a mutual understanding. I wish I could explain it better. The best I can do is to say there's an itch. And itches yearn to be scratched...

—Patrick

ONE

"He who makes a beast of himself gets rid of the pain of being a man."

Dr. Samuel Johnson; Writer

The rotund judge sat high on his bench as the bailiff handed him a piece of paper. Judge Elkins shifted his black robe that was caught on his sky-blue undershirt. He reached into his back pocket for a handkerchief to wipe the beads of sweat starting to build on his forehead.

It was September 4, 1969. The courtroom was hot that summer and barely moving fans did little to help push the air. There wasn't a whisper to be heard as everyone in the courtroom held their collective breath. A reporter standing in the back had his pad of paper in one hand and his pencil in the other. Like a loaded gun, his pencil would fire off the words "Guilty" or "Not Guilty," and he could run out the back door and shout it to the eagerly awaiting crowd on his way to the New Hope Post Headquarters. Reporters from Washington D.C. were in town to report the gory details that had been spoken out during the testimonies of various witnesses and police officers.

The walls of the courthouse had probably been a pearly white at one point, but over the years the color had soured to a dull, yellowish brown. The walls hadn't even been subjected to the horrors and crimes that big city courthouses have, but over the last few months there were plenty of things to overhear.

The mid-sized town of New Hope had been brought to its knees like never before. The likes of which the God-fearing farmers and their wives had never heard, much less seen. It had even garnered attention from the west coast all the way to the nation's capital. The words "pure evil" were being used in the same sentence as "serial killer" and "deranged psychopath." None of that bothered Patrick as he sat there without any emotion, deadpanning the world that right stared back at him.

"Will the defendant please rise?" Judge Elkins said aloud.

Patrick sat still and motionless with a cold and calculating look on his face.

"Mr. Fritz! Will the defendant please rise!?" the judge said, with vigor this time.

The distraught public defender shook Mr. Fritz by the arm and whispered into his ear, finally getting him to his feet. Patrick just shook his head and denied what was happening even though it was right in front of him. There was just one small thing—Patrick didn't exist. He was the deep-seated illusion of one, Arthur Fritz.

The judge opened the folded paper from the bailiff and tilted his head to see over his glasses, which he only used for his nearsightedness. His eyes scanned the document and didn't react to what he read, not that it was easy. The whole room studied his face, but like a good judge, he remained stoic.

"In the matter of the State versus Mr. Arthur Fritz. On the five counts of Murder One, the jury hereby finds you…"

The group of men and women sitting in the rows behind Arthur only wanted to hear one thing— guilty. They wanted him in the electric chair. Anything else would be a complete waste of time for themselves and the loved ones they had lost.

"Not guilty by reason of insanity. You are…"

"You sick son of a bitch! I hope you rot in hell!" a woman interrupted from the back. More conversations and chattering started as a result of the outburst, and before long the small but packed courtroom was in chaos.

"Order! Order in the courtroom!" Judge Elkins yelled as he banged on his gavel as hard as he could. Even though it was carved from the wood of a mighty oak, it was no match for the anger and forcefulness of Judge Elkins as it splintered in two and the head rolled across the hardwood floor. The wrathful mob of civilians froze in their spots. Judge Elkins, red-faced and scowling, pushed his white hair back into place.

"I will hold all of you in contempt! There will be order in my courtroom!"

The people, mad faced, reluctantly took their seats as to not get into further trouble. That was the difference between them and the man named Arthur Fritz. All the people in the room were deathly of afraid of having a contempt of court charge brought against them, even if they truly believed in something. And in this case, they did. In their minds, Arthur was more than mentally capable and knew exactly what he was doing. All the good people of the world wanted to get rid of all the bad people in the world. So they surrounded them and cornered them, wishing ill and hurt upon them. And when they couldn't kill them, they would exile them to distant corners of the world and lock them away in tiny rooms with cold walls, far away from the normal people of society. Far because they didn't want to be reminded that those dark and twisted souls were sewn from the same fabric as themselves. That only a minute piece of biology that they didn't understand could be in the wrong place, and that was all that separated the savages from the sane. Such was the case against Arthur Fritz. That was the difference. While the room returned to silence, Arthur still stood and faced his judge and jury.

"Mr. Fritz, you will hereby be turned over to the state for treatment, evaluation, and care at New Hope Psychiatric Hospital. This case is adjourned. That is all." He would have pounded on his gavel if he had one left.

Judge Elkins wore a look of disgust as he disappeared to his quarters for a drink. To hear what that man had done and to hear that he would be in a ward and not be executed was too much to handle. He was a judge, but he was still human. He wasn't scared of the things he had heard, no. What scared him was that someone was capable of doing them. Right here, in the peaceful and uneventful town of New Hope. Where things like this were never discussed, much less happened.

Patrick had the same look on his face as the judge, but not for the same reasons. Patrick was upset they were going away. The fun was over for now.

Or was it? Arthur slowly shifted his feet across the wooden floor as the chains allowed for only so much movement. His black and white jumpsuit had seen cleaner days. He wasn't even certain that it was washed before he received it. It smelled of dust and mothballs. There was a red stain from breakfast that morning where Arthur had spilled a drop of ketchup that he was putting on his scrambled eggs. Arthur didn't care where he was going, he just knew that Patrick would make sure he was safe and well taken care of.

The guards hauled him to the back door of the courtroom when people began leaving. At least Arthur didn't have to be alone. Even though Patrick wasn't in shackles and handcuffs, he followed him out and back into the holding cell until the transport from the jail to New Hope Psychiatric Hospital arrived. Appearing in and out of view, he never left Arthur's side. If he was anything, he was loyal. They both were. They were all they had.

Outside, the scene was on the verge of hysteria. How could the jury have come up with its decision? The mob couldn't comprehend the decision. They only saw red.

TWO

"You know, if I wanted to kill somebody, I'd take this book and beat you to death with it. And I wouldn't feel a thing. It'd be just like walking to the drug store."

-Charles Manson; Manson Family Cult Leader; Cincinnati, Ohio, USA

E ven though Arthur couldn't see it because the transport van had no windows, the building loomed vast and ominous, especially to an outsider. To the employees and groundskeepers, it was a place to call work and collect a paycheck. The cold brick structure stood tall among leafy trees. Big windows with bars lined the two-storied edifice, making it a cold place for someone to live out their days. It housed nearly one hundred of the area's insane. Some were from New Hope, but most of them from different parts of the surrounding area.

It would be a pleasant place to visit if it weren't for the disturbed tenants that rested inside the walls. New Hope Psychiatric Hospital was designed with a square base that included an outdoor courtyard area. Good behavior was rewarded with time outdoors. The green grass and fountain in the middle soothed the sometimes-agitated inmates, and the thought of watching the water gave them something to work toward. The hospital sat two miles from New Hope with nothing but trees and a few cottages in between. Only one road came in and out. During some winters, the staff would be stuck until the snow plows could get out there, leaving long periods and unrest between the staff and the patients.

All in all, New Hope Psychiatric Hospital took up about two and a half acres. It was two and a half acres of the most tortured souls the world ever knew. In 1960s New Hope, there were a few measures to keep them calm: electroshock therapy, drugs, and lobotomies. None were pleasant, but all took place within the thick walls.

★★★★★★★★★★

The transport van wobbled and shook as it left the smoothness of the paved road and hit the gravel-laden one that surrounded the facility. Since the hospital was receiving a celebrity in Arthur Fritz, the staff took extra precautions with security and placed Arthur in a secluded section of the hospital. All the preparations for a single inmate made them run out of daylight, as the sun sank behind the towering trees. However, all the other patients would be in bed so there would be less chance for anything to go wrong. The patients were susceptible to new people, and with Arthur's notoriety, it would be chaos.

There were no lights for miles around. The only way you knew you were at New Hope Psychiatric Hospital was from the tell-tale red light that shone out from the door of the processing entrance. Some of the staff joked that it was the entrance to hell. It glowed red and hot, inviting anyone that dared walked through the doors, willing or otherwise.

"All right, Arthur. This is home for the next however long," Douglas said through the air grate between the cargo area and the cab.

"Shit, this crazy loon probably doesn't even know where he is," Martin replied.

Douglas and Martin were both orderlies that did mostly transport-related chores and in-processing, not bad jobs for two black men in the 1960s.

"Wait up," Douglas said to Martin as he opened the door.

"Let me get a smoke man. I haven't had one all day," Douglas cried.

Martin nodded his head in agreement. It had been a long day getting ready for Arthur. Martin came around to Douglas's side of the large, white van. They both leaned on the vehicle while Douglas pulled out a crumpled pack of Camel cigarettes and handed one to Martin. With the sun fully asleep, their white uniforms glowed red from the light in the door.

"I haven't heard this guy say one word. You?" Martin asked, lighting Douglas's and his own cigarette.

"Naw, man. Quietest guy I've ever brought in here."

"I wonder what he's thinking? You believe he really did all those things they say he did?"

"Shit, man, I have to think so. Why else would he be here? You think they just made that stuff up?"

"I know, but damn. That's some repugnant shit. He looks so nice too," Martin noted.

The elder and wiser Douglas took a more serious look at Martin's remarks.

"I don't care how nice he looks, just remember what got him in here in the first place. You've only been here a year. Don't get attached to them. This is a hospital. They are here and not in prison because they're sick. Don't ever forget that," Douglas preached, pointing his long index finger at him.

"I know that," Martin said, looking down as if he disappointed Douglas.

Martin kicked some gravel around with his shoes before stomping out his smoke.

"Come on, man. Let's get this guy checked in," Douglas said.

Douglas unlocked the back doors with his driver's keys and swung the door open. There sat a man with thin brown hair and freckled arms. Arthur turned his head around to see the two orderlies starting at him. He felt like the sideshow at a carnival. His legs, tied with restraints to a metal hook attached to the floor of the van, kept him from moving. Martin had been right about him: he looked like a genuinely nice guy. One of the reasons Douglas was so good at his job was that he always treated the patients with respect. In his uneventful and tenured career, he found that it was always best to remain calm and to not get them riled up. He'd seen a few eruptions over the years, and they were never pretty. Some of the patients were strong, and when their sense of reality went missing, they became downright dangerous and quite powerful.

"Hey there, Arthur. You ready to get settled in?" Douglas asked.

Martin kept a few paces back and just watched. He was slightly star struck still from when they picked him up earlier. Again, Arthur said nothing. He just stared out into an invisible void. Douglas climbed up, undid the lock attached to the chains and gingerly reached at Arthur's shoulder and pulled.

"Be careful, Arthur. These vans are tall."

Arthur had what could only be described as a look of serenity on his face as he stared at his new surroundings. He stepped down from the van and moved his eyes toward the sky. The sun had finally set, and the stars showed their faces. An afterglow remained from the great presence of the sun, making it lighter near the horizon. Arthur took in a deep breath and closed his eyes. The country air was fresh compared to the stale stuff he had been breathing in the tiny county jail. Just as he released a long-held breath, a shooting star raced across the sky.

"You see that?" Martin said, with the innocence of a child.

"What are you talking about?" Douglas asked.

"A shooting star, man. It was right there. It went right over the roof."

"I saw it," Arthur said, smiling.

They both paused to stare at Arthur.

"Come on, Martin. We got a late night. Quit messing around."

Martin closed the van doors while Douglas led Arthur to the processing entrance. The red light from the vestibule glowed eerily while Arthur leaned up against the wall of the hospital and smiled. Patrick, Arthur's other devilish personality, could only smile because things were falling into place and Arthur was smiling because Patrick was. Who knows why they were really smiling, but Douglas wasn't going to bother him about it. There were lots of rules at New Hope Psychiatric Hospital, but no smiling wasn't one of them.

"Right through here, man. We're gonna get you a good room and then some breakfast in the morning. That all right with you?"

Arthur just shuffled his feet and made his way to the table where he would get his new clothes, inoculations, and some basic essentials for hygiene.

The interior of Arthur's new place was bland. Blank, pasty, off-white walls did little to help the décor. In the far corner of the temporary holding cell was a twin sized bed made of metal. The frame had chips of paint missing from where the previous occupant had nervously and constantly picked at it. Next to it was a small wooden nightstand. At the foot of the bed and against the other wall was a chest of drawers. And, for a place to focus and reflect, there was a small desk and chair next to the entrance. A dim hallway light flickered and popped loudly as another night shift orderly closed the door and locked it from the outside. The buzzing electricity could still be heard even after the door was closed.

Arthur sat down in the middle of the bed with interlocked fingers, his smile still beaming.

"Are you okay? You haven't said one word to me since we got here," Patrick asked Arthur. Arthur never responded.

Patrick walked around the room, studying the place, but mostly formulating a plan. Not only were the walls and locks a problem, but so was Arthur. Always Arthur. He had to be convinced of everything. But Patrick never seemed to have a problem with it before. Arthur laid down on the bed and slowly shuffled himself under the covers. The starchy white sheets were rough on his skin. They still had some residual detergent on them.

"I'm fine really. It feels good to be in a secure place. As weird as that sounds."

"Yeah, we have time now. Time to think about our next move in the grand scheme. Remember, this is a long game."

Patrick often talked of plans and schemes, but Arthur didn't like to get caught up in the details. Living in the moment was good enough for him. So was the mantra: In Patrick we trust.

"And what's our next move, Patrick?" Arthur asked.

"To find some zebras while we wait, Arthur," Patrick answered with a sly look on his face.

"Remind me of the zebras again, Patrick," Arthur said, letting on that he seemed like the rhetoric.

"Everyone out there in the world wants to be the lion, Arthur. They want to be king of the jungle. They want to growl and show their teeth. But none of them will kill the zebra. You saw them in the courtroom. When they found you not guilty they roared, they got loud. But did any of them bite? Not a one. But not us, Arthur. You and I. We bite...and we bite hard."

"But do we have to kill them, Patrick?"

"Yes, Arthur. We absolutely must kill them. It's how nature works. It's what we're programmed to do. Well, it's what I'm programmed to do. I'm the lion inside you. The world is our safari."

"So, what's the plan?"

"We have to tread lightly at first. We are going to have to learn how things work here. I must study the people. Not only the staff but the other patients. You know what they do to people in here, right?"

"No, I don't."

"Oh Arthur, you have so much to learn about the world. It's a good thing you have me."

Patrick was the smooth and charismatic one. He was the ultimate salesman that could get you anything you needed or didn't need. His clean-shaven look added to his dapper appearance. His slicked-back hair had a slight shine from the ambient light. As Arthur rested and closed his eyes, Patrick was hard at work. He paced the floors in the tiny room, scratching his chin to bring out the ideas. Patrick was a genius, but he rarely got the credit. Arthur always got labeled as the smart one. Not because of the way he spoke or his mannerisms, but

because hardly anyone knew about Patrick. Arthur
could have done without the notoriety; he was
merely along for the ride. It was Patrick's world;
Arthur was just living in it…literally.

THREE

"We've all got the power in our hands to kill, but most people are afraid to use it. The ones who aren't afraid, control life itself."

-Richard Ramirez; "The Night Stalker"; 25 victims; El Paso, Texas, USA

"**G**ood morning, Arthur. My name is Gladys. Did you sleep well?" she asked.

The door swung open slowly, and she peeked in cautiously. Gladys wasn't alone, she was accompanied by backup. Arthur wasn't to be taken lightly until the doctor had evaluated him and put him on some medication. Until that point, he was considered dangerous. He was a murderer. He was a sick and demented serial killer. No one at New Hope Psychiatric Hospital would be taken off their guard, making Patrick's job even harder.

"Oh, hello there," Arthur said, rising from the sheets like a ghost. His hair scattered about as if he had tossed and turned all night…which he had.

"Well, we have a busy day today, Arthur. We've got to get you fed, and you have an appointment with Dr. Benson."

Gladys was a middle-aged black woman with a deep southern accent that seemed to get worse the further north she went. With New Hope being tucked up near the border of Maine and New Hampshire, her accent was strong.

New Hope was named such because the settlers who moved up into northern Maine just after the colonies started to form had to retreat slightly further south because the harsh winters became unbearable. New Hope was just as its name described; it was shelter from the storm. A place to be optimistic. And now that Arthur was locked away inside the walls of the hospital, the town could return to that status. Safe. Lovely. Quaint. But nothing lasted forever. Things always changed. How long could these walls hold Patrick? Gladys wasn't going to take any chances — her guard was up.

"Arthur, beware of this one," Patrick said, sharply from the corner of the room.

"Why do you say that?" Arthur answered.

"Well, that's part of the process here, Arthur," Gladys said.

"Oh, I'm sorry. I wasn't speaking to you. I apologize for the confusion."

"Well, who are you talking to?" she asked.

"Patrick. He's right over there in the corner," he said, pointing to the blank spot opposite his bed.

"She's a wolf, Arthur. She's not to be messed with," Patrick continued.

"But she's so sweet and pleasant."

"I know, and that's why you need to watch it around her."

The three-way conversation was getting to be a bit much for Gladys. She had seen plenty of people talking to imaginary beings, but none as calm and as convincing as Arthur. Most twitched around, acting confused, but not this guy. He was so believable that, for a split second, she looked over her shoulder as to not be surprised by another guest in the room.

"We need to put some restraints on you, for the time being, Arthur. This is Jimmy. He's going to help me get the shackles on you. Is that all right wit' you?"

"Yes, Gladys. Go right ahead. I understand the need for restraint, but I can assure I'm not going to do anything."

"I believe you, but I show you my trust with the restraints," she replied.

"You see Arthur, she's not to be toyed with. Remember her. We have to profile everyone in here. That southern accent baaas like a sheep, but she's a wolf."

"Gotcha," Arthur replied.

"You talking to me or Patrick?" Gladys asked.

"It's Patrick. He's non-stop with his chatter today. I'm sorry."

Jimmy, the newest orderly at New Hope, was jumping into the water head first with Arthur. Frail, skinny, pale, Jimmy had only been there four weeks, and this was what he had to deal with.

"Go on, Jimmy. Like we practiced. Be real gentle," Gladys said, exaggerating the "real" part.

Her soothing, but strong and commanding voice made her a natural, take-no-shit kind of leader. Jimmy reluctantly slid into the room, got on his knees, and reached around Arthur's ankles while Arthur sat like the ideal cooperating patient on the bed. Patrick stood in the corner with his astute vision, never taking his eyes of Gladys. Arthur hadn't seen it, but there was a third person in the doorway. New Hope wasn't taking any chances on Arthur Fritz. Patrick's eyes flowed down from Glady's face and slowly down to her right hand, which laid gingerly in her white coat pocket. Inside was a large syringe loaded full of Etorphine, a drug powerful enough to neutralize an elephant, maybe even Patrick. A few of the doctors and Gladys carried it on them in the rare case of a patient slipping out of reality. The only difference this time was that Gladys was prepared and anticipated using it.

"Just let him do his thing, Arthur. We are in recon mode right now," Patrick said calmly.

As always, Arthur listened to Patrick and sat there patiently while Jimmy learned the ropes of restraining patients. When Patrick wasn't speaking to Arthur, he was speaking through him. Right now, Patrick let Arthur do all the talking, but he could intervene at any time.

It was clear why the new guy was on restraints, and the elder and wiser orderly stood back. She had the big guns. She had the great equalizer that could drop him like a sack of potatoes. Not only that, but she knew exactly where to place it. This new and powerful drug was being used across the nation in hospitals to subdue out-of-control patients.

Too much and it could stop their breathing; too little and they could easily overpower the staff.

Arthur sheepishly shuffled his feet along the cheap, lowest-bidder tile. Jimmy was in the front, leading the charge, and Gladys was in the back, like a wolf circling the flock. And never too far away was Patrick—Arthur's constant. Arthur's room was in the west end of the facility, just above the in-processing entrance. There were fewer rooms in that area, and the control was tighter. Patients like Arthur hadn't been vetted yet; they were still a bit of an unknown.

Natural sunlight was all that was needed to keep the hallways and rooms well lit. Plenty of light got in, even though all windows had the security wires built in between the thick panes of glass. The walls were nothing but cinder blocks painted the similar off-white coloring as the entire inside of the building. All in all, it was a bland and poorly thought out color scheme, but that was by design. You avoid whatever it takes to not get the patients roused. Especially the crazy ones...

"Right this way, Arthur. The section we're in now is called the Upper West Wing. This is a temporary place for you until Dr. Benson decides where you will be assigned. He's in charge around here. He's the boss. First, you have an appointment with Medical this morning after breakfast, then you have a pretty lengthy session with Dr. Benson."

Arthur didn't respond. He was busy watching Patrick peek into all the windows.

"Just a bunch of dopes in here," Patrick yelled out. His words had no echoes, mostly because they weren't said aloud, only in Arthur's twisted brain.

Jimmy moved ahead to open a door on the right. He pulled his keys out of his white coat pocket and unlocked the door. Releasing the keys, they flung back into his pocket on the attached line. Patrick immediately took notice of the keys. Jimmy was a liability, and Patrick could smell blood in the air. Just before Jimmy could open the door, ungodly screams came from far down the hall. The entire group stopped in their tracks.

"Ahhhhhh!" the voice yelled out. "They're coming for all of us! They put a radio in my brain!"

The screams were blood-curdling and seemed agonizing in nature. Scuffling sounds echoed as orderlies could be seen tackling and wrestling a poor man.

"Is he okay?" Arthur asked.

"He's okay. That's John. He thinks aliens from outer space are coming to get us all," Gladys said.

"Maybe they are…" Arthur smiled.

"Ahhh, you're jokin' aren't you, Arthur? I got my eye on you."

"And we have our eye on you, Gladys," Patrick whispered.

The temporary room they were in had one small table in the middle and a small metal door near the back. It was a dumbwaiter that connected to the kitchen so the staff could easily get food to the restricted patients on the second floor. Jimmy escorted Arthur over to the table and sat him down. Jimmy was quiet and reserved, but that was about to change. Patrick was ready to talk, but he always talked through the same body they shared...Arthur Fritz.

"How are you this morning Mr.??" Patrick asked hanging the question out there.

"Barnett. Jimmy Barnett. But you can call me Jimmy. I'm fine."

"Just fine Mr. Barnett? How long you been here?"

"A month or so," Jimmy answered and then immediately looked back at Gladys to get a visual indication that it was okay to be talking with him. She gave an ever-so-slight nod, indicating that he needed to learn to interact with the patients more.

"And do you like it? Do they treat you well here?"

"They do."

"Come on, Mr. Barnett. I won't bite. Loosen up. Tell me about yourself. We need to get to know each other. You're a young kid and if you stay here for many years like Gladys there and old Douglas...well, you'll be spending the best years of your life with me. We might as well enjoy them. Am I wrong?"

The way that Patrick put the story together made it hard for Jimmy to disagree with.

"I guess that's right."

"So, go on, boy. Tell me about yourself," Patrick pushed.

Patrick looked down at Jimmy's hands while they slowly began to tremble. Jimmy could sense that

"Arthur" saw his nerves show. Patrick just smiled warmly. He was getting to Jimmy, but that wasn't much of a challenge for Patrick. He was just warming up.

"Well, I live on a farm with my parents. It's a few miles down the road. I got tired of farming," Jimmy said, opening the dumb waiter to find a tin tray, a cup of milk and some plasticware carefully wrapped in a napkin. He brought the entire tray over and sat it in front of Patrick.

"Here you go," Jimmy muttered.

Patrick studied the tin tray intently. It had a larger concave dish filled with eggs and potatoes and three others along the side with Cream of Wheat, some sliced bananas, and a dried piece of toast. Patrick stared at the scratch marks on the tin and wondered how many deviants had this tray served. How long had it served as a tool to keep these people alive? The very same people that the town wanted nothing to do with. He wondered how much damage it could do to a human skull. But he showed restraint. Jimmy was weak, but not the reason they were here.

"You see, Arthur? You see what they do? They keep you alive, but kill you slowly all at the same time" Patrick said. "But not us. This place is our safe spot. They've done us a favor by putting us in here."

"Thank you, Mr. Barnett," Patrick responded.

It looked much better than it tasted. Powdered scrambled eggs and most likely freeze-dried potatoes. With the country at war in Vietnam and the U.S. in a space race with the USSR, quality goods and funding weren't going to mental institutions, they were going to technology and guns. As dangerous as Vietnam was, Jimmy had a better chance of finishing a couple of tours and coming home alive than he would of retiring and living a good life in New Hope with Arthur Fritz in the building.

"So, who helps your father and mother on the farm?" Patrick continued while taking a bite of the watery eggs.

"Oh, I have two older brothers that help, but not for much longer. My dad found some hired hands that can get more done than me. I didn't do so well on the farm, so I decided to try something new," Jimmy said, shifting his dirty blonde hair back into his right part.

Now Patrick was getting somewhere. Jimmy thought he was having a friendly conversation with a serial killer, but instead, he was being led to give information to a serial killer that he could use later.

"Well, that's admirable that you're branching out. But I must ask, why aren't you or your brothers in Vietnam?"

"My brothers did get drafted, that's why I said not for long. I got drafted as well but didn't pass my physical. I have a bum leg," he said, pointing at his left leg.

"I guess that's why I couldn't work as hard on the farm as my brothers."

"I could tell right away that you were a smart one. You knew your body wasn't going to get you places, but your brain was."

Jimmy just smiled. He was putty in Patrick's hands. Gladys just stared at the two conversing. She could tell that the demeanor of Arthur had changed. She didn't know it was Patrick talking, but this was all a consistent part of her job. She was just glad Jimmy was starting to come out of his shell. She had been worried he wasn't going to make it in this job. You couldn't be timid if you were going to work at New Hope Psychiatric Hospital.

"Oh, Arthur…?" Patrick called from the corner of the room. "I do believe we found a zebra. A weak and sick one that is starting to slow down the herd. What do you think?" Patrick said coyly.

As to not garner attention, Arthur put his head down and nodded in agreement while slurping up the cold Cream of Wheat with his spoon. He didn't have to answer for Patrick to know that he was on board.

"Good. Our young Jimmy here is about to learn some valuable lessons… I know you might not agree with me right now, Arthur, but you will see it one day. You will see that we are doing the world a great service. We are the conscious entity of nature that cannot be ignored. New Hope is our safari. It is our land, and we must show the other animals who it belongs to."

FOUR

"I was born with the devil in me. I could not help the fact that I was a murderer, no more than the poet can help the inspiration to sing."

-H.H. Holmes; Estimated 20–100 victims; Gilmanton, New Hampshire, USA

Arthur half-heartedly finished his breakfast in under an hour and was hurried along to the next event. He loved a home-cooked meal, but ever since being on trial and held in jail, he had gotten used to the bland food. Patrick had been keenly taking note of the layout and the personnel. The West wing was quiet, and hardly any people occupied it. The ones that did stayed locked in their rooms, isolated from the general population. Patrick would see an occasional face pressed up against the glass in the more restricted areas. The quiet halls were occasionally shaken up by a yell or a scream coming from the courtyard or lower floors. After scanning the area, Patrick concluded that Dr. Benson had his hospital under control and kept a tight ship.

"Arthur, this is Dr. Halcombe. He's our MD here. He oversees medicine and the physical health of our patients."

"Hello, Mr. Fritz. My name is Jeremy Halcombe. We're going to check you out today, is that all right?"

Dr. Halcombe spoke loudly as if Arthur was a deaf and dumb idiot like all the others around here. Clearly, he didn't listen to the news or wasn't a fan of current events.

"Arthur, tell him our hearing is fine," Patrick quipped.

Arthur let out a small laugh that the others in the rooms didn't seem to understand.

"After seeing a lot of patients, I have come to understand that I have cold hands. Go ahead and strip down, you can put your clothes there on the counter and take a seat here on this table for me," Dr. Halcombe said, pointing to a padded observation table with a thin piece of paper over the top of it.

Arthur took a seat as per the doctor's orders. Gladys stood like a watch dog in the corner of the room, ready to jump at any sign of danger.

Arthur slid the restraints over his sleeves and unbuttoned his shirt. He did the same with his pants, but Gladys had to undo the chains on his feet. Only wearing white boxer shorts and not afraid to bare it all, he pulled them down too and stood naked as could be. Gladys didn't bat an eye at the stripped Arthur. There was nothing she hadn't seen or heard here that would make her blush.

"Okay, Arthur. I'm going take a listen to your heart now," Dr. Halcombe said, leaning in and putting the stethoscope to Arthur's chest.

"Hey Arthur, we could break his neck right now if we wanted to," Patrick said softly.

"Maybe now's not the time," Arthur replied.

"Ahh, he has learned patience. I like this side of you, Arthur," Patrick replied.

"Excuse me?" Dr. Halcombe asked.

"Oh, nothing," Arthur answered.

"Well you have a healthy heart, Arthur," the doctor replied.

Something about a vigorous and rhythmic heartbeat soothes the old soul. While Dr. Halcombe continued his exam, Patrick kept talking away.

"Jimmy is our guy, Arthur. He's weak. We are doing him a favor," Patrick said.

"Okay, Arthur. We have a few inoculations to give you, but you seem fit as a horse," Dr. Holcombe said, taking off the blood pressure cuff.

Dr. Holcombe grabbed an oversized needle and filled it with a clear solution from a tiny little bottle.

"You'll feel a little pinch here, Arthur."

"You feel that, Arthur?" Patrick asked.

Arthur only winced as the big needle easily penetrated his skin.

"What they do to us will come back a million times worse on them. Grin and bear it."

"Okay, Arthur. We are done here. I'm going to update your chart, and you are off to your meeting with Dr. Benson. You have any questions for me?"

"No, Doctor. I'm looking forward to meeting him."

Patrick was foaming at the mouth to meet Dr. Benson face to face, but Arthur couldn't care less. To Arthur, he was just another person, but to Patrick, it was a chess match. He was anxious to match wits and see what this guy had. He wouldn't have to wait long either. Gladys and Jimmy led Arthur to the southeast corner of the building, the exact opposite corner of where Arthur and the other new arrivals were housed. While they casually walked down the hall, Patrick was stalking behind the group, just like a lion. Today, patience wasn't Patrick's strong suit. He was hungry. He wanted to eat. And very soon he would.

Dr. Benson's office was exactly like Arthur had imagined. A neat and tidy desk with a nameplate on the front, a pen, a perfectly aligned stack of papers, and a typewriter. Behind him was a locked filing cabinet and in front of the desk was a metal chair that was bolted to the floor. The metal was as cold as it looked. White walls surround it all. As cold as it appeared, Patrick saw it like an intimate setting. A place for an up-close-and-personal one-on-one with the good doctor. He could hardly wait.

"Go on, Jimmy. I can't be telling you how and when to do everything. Get down there," Gladys said with a harsher tone. Jimmy jumped at Gladys's command and shackled Arthur to the chair. Patrick just smiled. Jimmy was getting weaker and weaker, and soon he would need to be thinned from the herd. It was only a matter of time.

"Okay, Arthur. Dr. Benson will be here shortly. Just try to relax." Gladys said calmly.

"Thank you, Gladys," Arthur said politely.

As Gladys and Jimmy left the room, Arthur sat there patiently while Patrick paced small circles in the corner.

"You okay, Patrick?" Arthur asked.

"For once in my life, I'm anxious. We've been waiting a while to get in front of this guy."

"I know. Remember to have patience. That's what you tell me."

"Yeah. Yeah."

Just then the door clicked and opened slowly. In walked the slender and lanky man representing the age of late fifties. His glasses looked oversized for his face, and his hair was as thin and wiry as he was. Arthur concluded he looked overworked and tired, but he was in charge for a reason. He was a brilliant psychiatrist that deeply cared about healing and making the world a better place. Dr. Benson rushed in, adjusting his glasses on his noses and took a seat.

"Arthur Fritz. My name is Dr. Harold Benson," he said with newfound enthusiasm.

"Hello, Doctor. It's a pleasure to meet you."

Dr. Benson stared keenly at Arthur, trying to get a first impression of him. But Arthur gave him little to work with.

"I have to say, Arthur, my staff and this whole place were a buzz when we heard you were coming here. I, for one, am excited to work with you. It may sound insensitive, but I'm as eager as they are. Doctors in my profession rarely get a chance to meet someone as special as you."

"And what do you mean by someone like me?" Arthur replied.

"Well, they say you're a genius. They say you're incredibly smart."

"I don't know about all that. I'd say I'm a relatively normal guy."

"I don't believe 'normal' is the word that I'd use to describe you, Arthur. But I am curious to find out more. I could tell right away that you're an intelligent man. It's going to be a challenge to know what makes you tick. But from the evaluations and things I've read about you, yeah, I'd say you're a genius."

"I think you'll find that we agree on a lot of things, Harold. May I call you Harold?"

"Please, call me whatever you'd like."

"You want to make the world a better place. Yes?" Arthur asked.

"Yes, that's correct. I take it you heard of me then."

"I have. But you'll be glad to know that Patrick wants the same thing."

"Ah…yes. I've heard of Patrick. I'm sure we'll get to talking about him one day. But Arthur, you're in here because you've killed people. Do you understand that? That's not helping them. But I'd like to hear more about your position on how you think you're helping the world."

"That'll be for you and Patrick to discuss."

"And we come full circle back to Patrick. I read about him in your state trial evaluation, you know?"

Dr. Benson stood up from his chair proudly with his arms folded neatly behind his back. His beady eyes piercing right through the thick lenses of his spectacles. Judging. Always judging.

"You see, Arthur, in my profession there are two schools of thought on people like you. The first is that you are the way you are, and there is nothing that can be done. The other is that you know the difference between right and wrong. You simply fail to act on that information."

"And which school are you from?"

"The latter of course. I think you can be treated. So that begs the question; you know Patrick doesn't exist, right?"

"I know very well he doesn't exist….to you. But to me, he's here. He listens. He gives me advice. He's my friend," Arthur said, looking to the corner.

"Is he here, right now, Arthur?" Dr. Benson asked.

"He is indeed. He's standing right there," Arthur said, pointing his chin to the corner.

Dr. Benson took out a file from the stack and began to look through it. The talk of Patrick seemed to get him a little more excited.

"Is it possible to speak with him? I know it's early, but I'd like to meet him."

"What do you think, Patrick?" Arthur asked.

"Not right now. Let him talk. He's giving us a lot of information. Keep him talking," Patrick answered.

"I'm sorry. Harold. He's not in the mood to talk to you right now," Arthur said.

"I think that's just too bad. Maybe in our next session. So, Arthur, what can we do here to help you?"

"In what sense? I really feel fine."

"Well, you're a ward of the state. You aren't in prison, and you didn't get the electric chair because you need help. So, how can we rehabilitate you? Medicine? Shock therapy?"

"What makes you think I need help, Harold?"

"Oh? So, you don't think you're sick?"

"As I said, I feel fine. I can't help the fact that Patrick is here."

"Well, who killed those people?"

"Patrick did."

"Therein lies the problem, Arthur. He doesn't exist. You do. And you killed those innocent people, not Patrick. It's only you and me in this room."

Arthur sat patiently, not quite knowing what to say to that.

"Don't let him get to you, Arthur. He wants you to think I'm not here. But we both know that isn't true. Stay tough. He can't break us," Patrick said, gliding over to Arthur and whispering in his ear.

"You're a kind man, Arthur. I don't believe you committed those heinous murders. I don't believe that one bit. That's why we need to help you," Dr. Benson said with delicate care.

"You think I'm crazy, don't you?" Arthur asked.

Dr. Benson shuffled around in his chair, clearing his throat before standing up, presumably to give his speech on how the world views the people in his care.

"Arthur, the men in my field, don't like to use the word crazy here or anywhere. We…I am trying to change that wording and culture. Sick or disturbed is preferred. We are really trying to get into the mind of the patient so that we can fix what is wrong with them. It is believed that every malady of the mind can be cured."

"Harold, I understand that you and I are cut from a different cloth, but I don't know what you want from me."

"I want to get to know you. The real you. And Patrick too."

"What about what we want? How do we get that?" Arthur asked

"Well, what do you want?" Dr. Benson asked, moving back behind his desk to face Arthur.

"Something more…intimate. Something we couldn't get anywhere else. We want to get to know the real you, Harold."

"You want to get to know me eh? Well, I think you're here to get treatment. You are sick, Arthur. Killing people is not normal, and we are going to get real deep into it and see if we can get you help. There is a lot of new research on antipsychotic drugs. It's an exciting time in the field of psychiatry right now." Dr. Benson said, changing the subject and the tone.

"Tell him, Arthur. Tell him we won't be his guinea pig," Patrick said.

"You think I'm going to be your lab rat, Harold?" Arthur asked with his eyes squinted.

"No, Arthur, but I am committed to helping the patients here. And I will do whatever it takes to do that. Some patients require a full-frontal lobotomy. Some get better and level out on meds. It just depends. As we get to know each other, we'll see what works for you. I think right now we are going to start off with some pills, see how they make you feel. Should just mellow you out. You'll be fine."

"We can't accept that as an answer, Arthur. Fight back!"

"Oh, Harold, do you just fix the world by giving out zombie pills? Is that how you do it? What happened to good old-fashioned head shrinking? You're better than this, Harold."

"Oh, don't get me wrong, Arthur. You are my main case here. I've been waiting a long time to get you in that chair. But we have to take the danger away. The pills will do that. You're a smart guy, surely you understand this."

"Oh, I understand it perfectly, Doctor. I have a funny feeling that you and I are going to get to know each other more than you can ever imagine." Patrick uttered his final words before disappearing. He realized Arthur could only be pushed so far before tiring out.

Dr. Benson scribbled some notes into Arthur's file and scheduled his next appointment. Patrick wasn't pleased, but he knew from the beginning this was going to be a long game. Patrick observed and finally spoke out to Arthur.

"It's okay Arthur, you did well."

"I just don't like to fight," Arthur said aloud.

"Excuse me?" Dr. Benson said, looking up from his writing.

"Oh, I was talking to Patrick."

"Okay. But sooner or later he's going to have to talk to me."

"He will Harold, I assure you. He's excited, but right now is not the time."

"Very well. I am going to get you on some meds and move you to a single cell downstairs and mix you in with the general population. You think you can behave? If you hurt someone, there will be consequences, Arthur. There are many, many more options for wellness that we can take. We got a basement full of scary stuff that will get you right…one way or the other."

"You won't have a problem with me, Harold."

"Good. Then I will see you in a few days for a follow-up, and we will begin to...get to know each other. Sound good?"

"Sounds great, Harold. I'm looking forward to our sessions."

"Same here, Arthur."

Dr. Benson looked up at the clock. He had to hold himself back from digging too deep. He had been following the murders and the trial, eagerly awaiting Arthur's arrival to his hospital. He had big plans of his own with Arthur.

Gladys escorted Arthur out of Dr. Benson's office and back into his holding cell. It had gone exactly as Arthur and Patrick had planned it. Dr. Benson understood that Dr. Benson was in charge, and that was part of the illusion. That was part of the big plan they had boiling up. Today things were calm and quiet, but all that was about to change very, very soon. The lion yawned and stretched his back legs. He hadn't eaten in a while, and he was getting hungry. Very, very hungry...

FIVE

"You feel the last bit of breath leaving their body. You're looking into their eyes. A person in that situation is God!"

-Ted Bundy; 36 victims; Burlington, Vermont, USA

Back at home in his study, Dr. Benson poured himself some bourbon while a bouncing and lively Cornelius came running up. Cornelius was a three-year-old Tabby with a magnificent orange coat with a few white stripes running down the back. He was a good cat who spent a lot of time outside getting birds and mice, but when Dr. Benson was home, Cornelius was right there by his side. On weekends when Dr. Benson would watch TV or work from home, there he was. He'd even sleep on top of the desk while Dr. Benson wrote in his patient records or his prized manuscript for his book on how to treat the criminally insane.

"How is Mr. C. today? Huh? How's my man?" The only answer was a loud meow.

"Me? Well, I met with Arthur today," Dr. Benson said, letting himself melt into his posh chair.

"This is the one, Cornelius. Arthur is going to make us. I will make contact with the publishers in D.C. soon, and they will anxiously be waiting to hear back from me. Of that I am sure. Not very many people get to study a person like him. But we do. And he's exactly what I need…"

Cornelius waltzed a couple of figure-eights between Dr. Benson's legs before jumping on his lap. He didn't know of the doctor's plan, but he seemed to approve. Dr. Benson had only been sipping the bourbon, this time he took it all down in a big gulp with a confident, but nastily curled upper lip. This was his dream. This was his destiny: to be the most famous doctor the world has known. The one that treated Mr. Arthur Fritz.

★★★★★★★★★★

A few days had passed since his arrival, and Arthur was settling into his new cell. It was quite a bit smaller, but the size didn't bother him, and neither did the medication that Dr. Benson had prescribed.

"Please, take a seat, Arthur. Gladys, please shackle him. Thank you," Dr. Benson ordered.

"And how are we feeling today, Arthur?" he asked as Gladys shut the door.

"Okay, I guess. I feel…"

"Different?" Dr. Benson interrupted.

"Yes, but in a good way."

There was a calm and stillness to Arthur's voice that Dr. Benson hadn't heard the first time. He smiled in knowing that the first step to getting to Arthur was taking away his need to kill.

"Good, Arthur. I think you'll find it comforting to know that it can help you. We here at New Hope can help you. Truly, that's all we want."

Dr. Benson presented a warm smile on the outside while Patrick was smiling on the inside.

"He has no idea, Arthur," Patrick said from the corner.

"I know," Arthur responded.

"Good. Keep the act up. It's working," Patrick said.

"Is that Patrick you're talking to, Arthur?" Dr. Benson asked.

"Yes. He's right over there. But he's mad at you. He's mad at me for taking the pills."

"You see, they're making him weak. But we will get to the bottom of Patrick and where he came from. I will help you to understand why he's such a bad influence in your life and how he caused you to end up in here."

Dr. Benson jotted down some more notes in Arthur's file and shifted his hair over to the right side of his head.

"So, Arthur, I want to talk about what we started to talk about a few days ago. You said something about wanting to help the world. And I mentioned you were killing them and it wasn't helping them. Let's talk more about that."

Arthur shifted as best he could while chained to the chair. His brown hair parted neatly and laid to one side. His loafer style shoes perfectly pointing straight ahead, toward Dr. Benson.

"Well, to be honest, that's really Patrick's department."

"But you realize you killed people, right? You realize that it's wrong to do that?"

"I know it's wrong to do it, yes."

"But you did it anyway."

"Well, the way Patrick puts things, it's hard to argue with him."

"May I speak with Patrick now?"

Arthur looked over to the corner to see Patrick standing there in his jeans and long-sleeve work shirt. He leaned on the wall with a coolness of a popular high schooler.

"He said he's not ready to talk to you right now, but soon you will get to know him. And trust me, he's excited to talk to you as well," Arthur said.

"Very well. Then how about we talk about you, Arthur? Tell me about your childhood? Where did you grow up?"

Patrick rolled his eyes at the textbook psychiatry that Dr. Benson was trying to use.

"I grew up in upstate New York. Essex County to be exact, Harold. I guess you could say I had a fairly normal life growing up. My father was a hard-working man. He was in the second world war.

Helped fight the Japs. Mother stayed home and raised us."

"Us?" Dr. Benson asked.

"Me and my brother. Paul."

"Ah. keep going," Dr. Benson said, scribbling on his paper, taking meticulous notes.

"Father came home one day from the war, and things were never the same after that. He was quiet and stared at the wall a lot. Mother never fully recovered either. She tried to get him to snap out of it, but he never did."

"Tell me about Paul."

"Paul was three years older than me. Handsome and popular guy. He was a baseball star at the school and was headed for college to play in the big leagues one day. He died in a car accident one night his senior year. Father put a gun in his mouth a month later. I guess it was all too much for him."

"I'm very sorry, Arthur. But you're doing very well in opening up with me."

Patrick kicked his feet on the floor. If he had any compassion for anyone, it was for Arthur. Maybe it was the reason he was so protective of him. Maybe it was the reason he existed in the first place.

"It was just Mother and me after that. A few years after I left high school she died as well. I've heard it was from a broken heart."

Arthur's tone remained the same throughout the sad story of his childhood. Even Dr. Benson seemed to be a little saddened by his past.

"Do you think part of your childhood had anything to do with the creating of Patrick?"

"I don't believe I created Patrick. He came to me one day. Been like that ever since."

"You see Arthur when something traumatic happens to the mind, it fractures. It needs to cope with something it can't understand. Your mind created Patrick to deal with your loss. The problem arises when Patrick controls you. And it is obvious that he is out of control."

"But I feel fine, Harold."

"I know you do. Is there anything else you can think of?"

Arthur tilted his head toward the ceiling and cocked his neck.

"Hmmm. Maybe."

"Go ahead. What is it?"

"When Dad was off fighting the Japs, our neighbor, Mr. Dale…"

"Who was Mr. Dale?"

"He was a tall, lumbering man. Not many of the townspeople cared for him, and all the kids were afraid of him. In the summers when it would get hot, I remember he would sit on his porch wearing overalls with no shirt or underpants. The hair on his shoulders and back was bushy, popping out of the sides of his tight, blue overalls. And the tobacco. He would chew on a plug all day. Sometimes he'd spit it out on his shoes. Other times it just ran down his chin and onto his chest hair. Occasionally he would call Paul and me over to help him do chores and whatnot. After Paul got older, he stopped going over, and it was just me. Mr. Dale used to take me to his shed in the back yard. He'd give me candy to do things."

"What kind of things?"

"Like chocolate and hard candy."

"No, what kind of things would Mr. Dale ask you to do?"

"I vaguely remember him make me reach into his pocket and find a penny…eh…it was a long time ago Harold. I just…I don't know."

"That's enough for today, Arthur. I think you did fine. The medication is working great on you, and we have a lot of things to dig through. We are going to get to the bottom of Patrick and all your issues."

"Horse shit Arthur! Didn't nothing ever happen to you in that shed! Tell him to get to the real stuff," Patrick said, redirecting the conversation.

"Dr. Benson…" Arthur said in a deep and disappointed tone.

"Yes?"

"When are we going to get to the meat and potatoes? The real stuff?"

"Oh…Okay, Arthur. Let's talk real stuff then," Dr. Benson said, pulling out a large file from his desk drawer. Dr. Benson started rifling through the pages, and he stopped at one place in particular and winced.

"I have to say, Arthur. I read through the file a few times already, and it never gets easier to read. The pictures never get easy to look at it."

"Oh, you must be reading the police file. Good stuff."

"Tell me about Marvin Monte. Your first victim."

"Now we're getting somewhere, Harold," Arthur said smiling, knowing he pleased Patrick.

"How did you meet Marvin?"

"Marvin wasn't the first person we killed, Harold."

"I'm confused. Then who was? The file says he was."

"Yes, the file does say that, but that doesn't mean it's the truth. And since I've already been found to be guilty by reason of insanity, then that's all that matters. Am I right?"

"I guess so."

"Also, anything I tell you in here falls under doctor–patient confidentiality rules. Isn't that right too?"

"Yes, it is. I see you've done your homework."

Dr. Benson was a bit shocked to learn that Arthur wasn't as green as he let on, but he still felt in control. This was his hospital and Arthur was still his patient under his care. That was the most important thing to Dr. Benson.

"So, Arthur, then tell me who your first victim was."

Arthur sat perfectly still in his cold, metal chair. He stared awkwardly at Dr. Benson for a few seconds before answering.

"She was an old lady named Martha Denison. She lived on the land next to mine. Martha had a small house about a mile down a dirt road from mine. I would take her loads of wood and checked in on her from time to time. She didn't have any family left, and her husband died a while back. Martha had started to develop some form of mental impairment as the years wore on."

"How do you know this?" Dr. Benson said, taking notes.

"She would repeat herself continually. Sometimes she didn't know who I was. I could see the changes in her. It looked like the life was slowly leaving her body. I could tell she was suffering."

"So, you killed her?"

"It wasn't that easy, Harold. I just didn't wake up one day and decide to kill her."

"Well, what happened?"

"Patrick killed her. Well, it was his idea. He convinced me we needed to do it. That we were doing her a favor. That she was suffering. And she was."

"Interesting. So, you actually killed her, but Patrick made you do it?"

"I wouldn't say he made me do it."

"What would you say then?"

"I'd say he made me understand why we needed to."

"And why did you both need to?"

"That, you'll have to talk to him about. He's the one that knows."

"Arthur, I've been asking to talk with him. When is he going to come out and be a man?"

Patrick scoffed from the corner of the room as he studied Dr. Benson intently.

"When he's ready, Harold. That's all I can tell you. He's a finicky guy."

"And how will I know when I'm talking with him, Arthur?"

"You'll know by seeing subtle changes. He's more confrontational. His voice deepens a bit. Oh, and he chooses to use last names. For instance, when I call you Harold, he'll call you Dr. Benson. I take it to be that Patrick is just old fashioned in that sense. But yes, that is a tell-tale sign of who you're talking to."

Dr. Benson wasn't surprised at the way Arthur talked about Patrick. Invisible people and split personalities were nothing new to him. What surprised him was the calm demeanor of Arthur and the documented ugly and violent side of Patrick. Dr. Benson still felt in total control, but deep down all he wanted was to converse with Patrick. He wanted to get to the root of the problem. He had big ambitions that rested with Arthur Fritz and company.

"So, tell me what happened with Martha, Arthur."

"Not much to tell, really. We went over there one day, and she was laying in the bathroom. She said she had been there for two days, but really, who knows how long it was. She wasn't exceptional at keeping track of time. I'll never forget her old, naked body lying there. It was quite disturbing."

"Yeah, I could see that. Looking at old people naked isn't very flattering. What happened next?"

"We pulled her up from the floor and moved her into her bed. She said she was hungry and that she hadn't eaten in a month. I tried to tell her that she would be dead if she hadn't eaten in a month, but it was no use trying to reason with her. After we had got her in the bed, I built a fire in the living room…the house was cold. I gave her some water and told her I was going to go into the kitchen and cook her some eggs and bacon and that Patrick would stay there with her to make sure she was alright. I could hear them talking. Patrick even made her laugh a few times."

"So, you went to cook, eh? What happened after she ate?"

"Patrick pulled me into the next room. It was a bedroom she had converted into a sewing room. Clothes and half-done blankets everywhere. He said he wanted to talk to me."

"What about?"

"About Martha. He said that she had told him she was suffering and that she just wanted to die.

He told me she went on and on about not knowing where she was and what she was doing."

"And did you believe him? Or do you think he just wanted to kill her?"

"I believed him. Poor Martha wasn't doing well at all. Especially after that fall. I'm surprised she even survived that."

"So, then what?" Dr. Benson asked.

"We worked out a plan to help her out, you know, give her what she wanted."

"And how did Patrick convince you that this was okay?"

"He said he could hear her soul talking to him and that my spirit animal was the lion. He said that he was the manifestation of that animal."

"Interesting. A lion huh?"

"Yup. I laughed at first, but he explained how lions work. How when they kill, they are helping the herd killing off the weak or the sick ones. He said that Martha was ill, and it was a natural thing."

"And what do you think? Do you think it's a natural thing?"

"Yes, I do. She was suffering. Can you not see that?"

"Oh, I know she was suffering. That's not my point. My point is why do you think you or Patrick are the ones who make that decision? You aren't God you know."

"I know we aren't God, but Patrick could hear their souls talking to him. It's what they wanted."

"I see. Well, Arthur, I'm glad you are here because you are in the right spot. We have so much to work with here. But I have to know how you did it. Will you finish the story of Martha?"

"Sure. As I said, we fed her a good breakfast. I don't think she had eaten that well in a long time. While she was in the bed eating, Patrick told me his plan on how we were going to help her out. He said I had to trust him that it would be quick and painless. I told him that I wouldn't do it if it weren't. So, I trusted him and followed his lead. He took over from there."

"Care to elaborate?"

"I wish I could Harold, but Patrick has all the details."

"Well, can he tell you and then you tell me? He's in the room, right?"

"Oh, he's here…yes, but he'd prefer to tell you properly and in the right way."

"What's the right way?"

"From his point of view."

"And how do we do that if he's unwilling to talk?"

"You'll meet him soon enough, Harold."

"You keep saying that, Arthur."

"One final question."

"Go ahead," Dr. Benson said, slightly frustrated.

"How long can someone live without eating?"

#

"I wish you all had one neck and that I had my hands on it."

-Carl Panzram; 21 victims; East Grand Forks, Minnesota USA

Arthur was placed in a corner cell so that he could be among the other patients, but more secluded at night. He was fine with this arrangement. It gave him the opportunity to be social during the day, and it gave it him the chance to be alone with Patrick at night.

Arthur trudged down the hall, looking for something to do. He had previously made the rounds through the building, so there wasn't much else to look at. The courtyard was still too cold to be opened. He stood in front of the door to his cell and stared at the itchy, gray blanket that was neatly folded on his bed. He was a bit of a slob, so he smiled when he realized that Patrick must have folded it. As neat and comfy as the bed looked, Arthur decided that the rec room had more interesting things going on.

The television volume seemed to be as loud as it could go when Arthur walked into the room. The Twilight Zone was playing, and nearly half the people in there were glued to the screen. The rest were either staring at the walls, or off into space, or sleeping where they sat. Heavy medication in large doses will have that effect. As Arthur entered the room and stopped in the entryway, another patient approached him.

"Hey there, ya patsy!" the man yelled.

"Hello."

"What's your name? You're new here aren't you, Friend?" the man laughed with a hoarse and raspy voice.

Arthur studied the man who appeared to be in his late fifties. He had a face full of white stubble, and one of his eyes seemed to be closed, or barely open, Arthur couldn't tell which. Not only was the man's appearance rough and ragged, but he stunk to high hell. None of it bothered Arthur. He was just his usual, soft-spoken self.

"I'm Arthur," he said, extending his hand.

"Well hell, Arthur. That was the name of my old math teacher. He died."

"I'm sorry to hear that," Arthur replied.

"I'm not. Son of a bitch flunked me! Ha, ha, ha!" The old man was crass and rude, but Arthur liked him.

"What's your name, Friend?" Arthur asked.

"I'm George. Old Crusty George is what they call me!" George said, slapping Arthur quite hard on the arm. "Whatcha in for, Art?"

"You mean you haven't heard of me?"

"Who are you, the prince of fuckin' Wales!? Eh?" George's hoarse laugh echoed in the room.

"Not exactly. But if you don't know me then you have no judgments against me. And I have none of you. Isn't that the best way to start a relationship?"

"As long as you're not an asshole, Art. There are plenty in here; we don't need anymore. I've been here since the place opened. That fucker, Benson, has tried every medicine they make on me, but I don't give a shit."

"What did you do?"

"They wanted to fry me, Art. Goddam fuckers wanted to fry me. You want a smoke?"

"No, thank you."

George took a cigarette from the front pocket of his dirty and half-ragged pajama-style outfit, and offered it to Arthur, despite him already saying no.

"No, thank you. I don't smoke."

George popped the filterless Camel into his mouth, walked over to the orderly, and asked him for a light. The patients could smoke in the building, but they weren't allowed to carry matches or a lighter for obvious reasons. George sucked in on the cigarette and let out a large plume of smoke into the air, most of it directed at Arthur's face. It wasn't intentional, but then again it kind of was. But that was George. He just didn't care.

"George, can I ask you a question?" Arthur said.

"Go ahead, ya patsy."

"What do you think of young Jimmy over there?" Arthur asked, pointing with his eyes.

"He's a Nancy Boy. I could take him."

"In a fight, sure. You look strong, but I mean what's his story?"

"He's weak. I'd love to kick his ass. Yours too!" George said, laughing hard before it turned into a nasty cough.

"That's what I thought too. Interesting. So, you like to fight George?"

"Anyone. Anywhere. I used to fight those pussies on the boat when I was in W-W-2. Not this weakling kind of boxing either. Bare knuckle. You spit your teeth out and keep fighting. See this droop eye? Got punched by a man twice my size. I got back up and nearly killed him after! Not like the patsies today. Wrappin' their hands in cotton and what not. I'll take 'em all!" George yelled with his fist flailing in the air.

"Calm down, George," Jimmy said from across the room.

"I'm calm, Jimmy boy."

"I'm sorry, Jimmy. I didn't mean to get him worked up," Arthur said.

Jimmy walked over from the checker table and stopped in front of them.

"It's not your fault. George just wants to fight everyone. Don't you, George?"

"I'll even fight these damn gooks in Nam. Little patsies compared to the Japs. The Japs were willing to die!"

"George, relax. Let's sit you down over here by the TV. Watch some Twilight Zone," Jimmy said softly.

"Arthur?" Patrick asked from the couch, with a lollipop in his mouth.

"Yes?"

"Jimmy dies tonight."

"I know."

★★★★★★★★★★

March 29, 1967

It's been two days, and I finally worked out a plan for Mrs. Denison. Arthur agreed to it as long as it would be quick and painless. He's nervous, but I'm talking him through this. Besides, this is what she wanted. This is why I'm here. In time, Arthur will learn to understand and appreciate these things.

We left Arthur's house around nine in the morning. It was a frosty morning, but the weatherman on the radio called for a high of sixty-five. Unusually warm this time of year, but the timing couldn't be better. The old dirt road to Mrs. Denison's house was an easy drive. The tall evergreens were sprinkled in between the bare-leafed oak and maple trees. It made for a beautiful contrast. I absolutely love this weather. While Arthur drove, I focused on giving Mrs. Denison the best care I could. I thought about that and my latest obsession, death. I believe that it goes hand in hand with my new-found job. That's what I've named my calling. Being a lion is a dirty job, but it is necessary. It must be done at all costs to keep the balance.

Most people don't like to think about death. It scares them. It presents an element of life that they can't control. I picture an egg inside of a young and fertile woman. That egg is met with sperm that is on its mission to find it. When they meet, the cell begins to divide and its built-in programming, which the scientists these days are calling DNA, tells the cells how and when to divide and what to become next. Quite elegant if you ask me. Back to the point, the life form has a strong desire to survive. But prior to that, it was all right. It didn't want life. It didn't need anything. It was fine before in the state that it existed in. What I'm saying is that it didn't ask for life. And the same goes for us. We didn't ask for death. But it's coming. To each and every one of us. Perhaps this is why I'm so fascinated with it. It's a destiny that you know is coming.

Mrs. Denison's house looked dark today. Maybe in some weird connectedness of all things, it knew I was coming. Between Arthur, myself and Mrs. Denison, Arthur seemed to be the most shook up. Mrs. Denison welcomed us in as though she hadn't seen us in years, but I could tell from her eyes that she still wanted me to help her out. When Arthur turned around to shut the door behind us, she winked at me. I took this to mean our arrangement was still on. I offered to make us all a pot of coffee, while I sent Arthur out to get the stump and ax out of the truck. I instructed him to take it into the woods just south of her house. Last time we were here delivering wood, I found a little trail that went into the trees, finally landing in a clearing. The stump wasn't very heavy. It was maybe twice the size of a dinner plate and only about 8 inches thick. The amount of dedication and focus I am giving is unbelievable. I spent the entire day before sharpening the ax. I wanted everything to be perfect for my first time. I overlooked no detail. By the end of the day, the ax was so sharp it would split hairs. It took me a while to get our all the nicks and burs that Arthur had put in it from missing his swings. I, on the other hand, was a crack shot. I took great care to oil and sand the handle too. It was smooth. It would slide between your hands easily now. This was about Mrs. Denison. This was about giving her the best care I could, the care she deserved.

—Patrick

SEVEN

"Let the torture and suffering in me end."

-Ronald Gene Simmons; 16 victims; Chicago, Illinois USA

April 04, 1967

I peeked out the window to see Arthur tucking the stump under his arm and laying the ax over his shoulder. While he did that, I poured a cup of coffee with two sugars, just like she preferred it. I asked her if she felt hungry, but she said no. A warm cup of coffee on a brisk morning as a final meal seems fair and fitting to me. I'm not sure what I'd want as mine. That day will come, I suppose. And here comes death, always back into my thoughts. While we waited for Arthur to set things up, I watched Mrs. Denison sip on her coffee and stare at the wall. Her inner voice was talking to me though. It told me she was ready and that she wanted to wear her favorite coat that Samuel had given her. She told me it was packed neatly in a box at the back of the closet. She couldn't remember the last time she had worn it, but she mentioned that it must have been waiting for this moment. I found the box just as she had described. I took the lid off, and the smell of moth balls was strong, but it was worth it. The white fur coat looked brand new.

I took the box back into the kitchen to find Arthur standing in the doorway. He didn't say a word. He just gave me the nod that everything was in place. I walked behind Mrs. Denison and held the beautiful fur coat for her to slip into. It was white with a few light brown stripes running down the back. I think of the poor animal that had to die for a human's vanity. Man can be such an awful beast. What is the mechanism that takes us from being animals to being cruel? Is being this intelligent worth the pain we endure? I'm not so sure of that answer anymore. Mrs. Denison stood up. She knew it was her time and she was ready. I mean, after all, this was her idea, but her wishes and my calling were no accident. I wrapped the fur around Mrs. Denison, and she took one final sip of the coffee. She hadn't even drunk a quarter of it, and it was still piping hot. I could see the steam rising from the cup. Arthur held the door open, and Mrs. Denison shuffled her feet slowly toward it. A chilly spring breeze swept in. I could see her shiver and her old rattling teeth started to chatter. At the rate she was walking, she would freeze to death before making the quarter mile hike into the woods. Mercifully, I lifted her over my shoulders and hauled her out. She seemed to enjoy the ride. Kicking her legs in excitement like a child being carried around by an adult. And with her mental state, that is very much what it was like.

The well-worn trail came to an end in the pale grass-covered clearing. The sun was peeking through the trees and like a spotlight on the leading actor, it lit up the stump that Arthur had beautifully placed. To top off the magnificent movie set, the ax leaned against the tree at the edge of the clearing on the north side. Ironic that the handle of the ax came from trees and the metal was forged by heat from a wood-burning fire; man, taking the beauty of nature and turning it into destructive items. But like the apes, we must use tools to survive. I put Mrs. Denison back on her feet gently, and she looked around, appearing a little lost. On the outside, she was a little disoriented, but on the inside, she was calm and ready. We must have stood in that opening for a good five minutes just staring at the layout. There is beauty in simplicity. It was like a scene from a Shakespearian play.

Mrs. Denison was starting to get a bit agitated. I think she was picking up the bad vibes that Arthur was putting out. I reassured her that everything was okay and that it was time. We walked over to the stump, and I told her to lay down in front of the stump. I couldn't help but appreciate how beautiful the cut wood was. The sharp chainsaw teeth left a smooth finish. While the sun lit up the stump, I had caught myself being carried away with counting the rings. I got to forty-three before Mrs. Denison's soul reminded me to do my job. It had been my first time, so I must confess that I was a bit nervous. Not because of what needed to be done, but because I wanted to do it right. This is an important job.

She laid down easily enough. I told her that she was going to take a nap and everything would be fine. Not everyone loves death that way I do. When you tell the physical body it's going to die; it reacts in a way that is not conducive to what the soul wants. This is what she wants. I reiterate that here because she tells me so. These memoirs are a documentation of that.

The time finally came. I think she is the bravest person I've ever met. Mrs. Denison asked me where we were. I told her that she was getting a check-up at the doctor's office and needed to lay very still. I stroked her old, sun-kissed skin and delicately brushed her hair back behind her ears. Her liver spots contrasted off her white, pale face. I put her arms across her chest and finally stood up. Arthur stood some feet back with what could only be described as a look of horror on his face. Now that it was time, he looked as though he wasn't ready. But not me. With a confident strut, I walked to the tree and grabbed the tool of the trade. Good ole' hickory. Hard as the day is long. The edge of the blade was true, cutting my finger when I stroked it across to check. I put my finger in my mouth and sucked out the blood. Blood always has had a distinct flavor to it. Always thick, but dull.

As Mrs. Denison lay motionless, I thought back to all the logs I split. The hits were always clean and dead center, leaving the now two pieces of wood to fall on each side. Would her head do the same? I

approached her from above while her feet were
pointing toward Arthur. His look of horror turned
to anxiety because it felt like I could feel his
heartbeat. Maybe I could. Three feet away and I
came to a stop and moved my head back straight
up to look through the tall trees at the blue sky.
"Any final words, Mrs. Denison?" Her soul only
replied with "Set me free, Patrick." And so, I did. I
took a mighty swing. The ax handle slid perfectly
between my dry hands on my backswing. And
with the ax at the apex of the swing, directly above
me, I compressed my knees to unleash the energy
like a loaded spring. Right between the eyes, I split
her head open like a ripe melon. It was glorious. The
blade went clean through and stopped in the wood
with a mighty thump. Mrs. Denison was no
longer. But in the cold air, I could swear I saw her
soul rise out above her body and thank me. I only
nodded my head in knowing that I did my job.
Like an artist who flicked his brush after painting
a masterpiece, I barely even noticed that a streak of
blood went diagonally across my face from the
blow. Some of it undoubtedly went into my
mouth. It tasted...different. It was full of life. It
spoke to me on a level I hadn't experienced. This is
how a lion must feel after a meal; completely
satisfied.

Arthur took good care of disposal and clean up. I
needed to be alone with my thoughts after what I
just experienced. Arthur struggled to pull the ax
from between the pieces of her head. I might have
put more force behind that blow than any others.
While he wiggled the ax free, I couldn't stop

thinking of what I had just witnessed. It's one thing to see something die, it's another to see its soul release right in front of your eyes. And that is precisely what I saw. It moved me to no end. It made firm the decision I had made to take on this calling. I will not fear death and, even more, I will look it in the eyes. I'm hopeful for what the future brings.

—Patrick

****

While Dr. Benson scurried around his office, putting even the slightest things that were out of place back to their designated areas, he pondered some basic questions about Arthur. Was Arthur Fritz simply playing dumb? He didn't think so, but the fact remained that he had gotten caught by the authorities. His sidekick was incredibly smart, so how did he allow that to happen? He wondered if it was what they wanted. Dr. Benson didn't think that was the reason, but he just couldn't find the answer. While still feeling in control, the smallest and ever so subtle whimper of doubt crept in, like a thief in an unguarded harbor. Losing control wasn't his métier, so he managed to shake it off quickly and moved passed it.

Interrupting his long train of thoughts on where all of this was going, the phone seemed to shake in place from ringing.

"Dr. Benson?" Gladys asked through the phone.

"Yes, I'm here, Gladys."

"You asked about Arthur. He's in the rec room."

"What's he doing? Is he alone?"

"No, he's talking with Jimmy."

While Dr. Benson tried to figure out Arthur and his future plans, Arthur sat in the rec room at a corner table and chatted up poor Jimmy. Arthur was positioned like an astute listener, so close to Jimmy that their shoes nearly touched under the small, round table. While Arthur did the talking and probing of information, Patrick was nearby doing the gathering and processing.

"So, tell me about your farm, Jimmy," Arthur prodded.

"Not much to tell, Mr. Fritz. Just a maple farm handed down from my grandparents and probably their parents."

"Oh, Jimmy, please call me Arthur. Last names are so formal."

"Sure, Arthur."

"What about your parents? You're the youngest of three, right?"

"Yes, sir. I was the runt growing up. That's what they called me anyways. Could hardly even use the machinery, I was so small. My damn leg always gave me problems. Both Dwayne and Bobby never really quit making fun of me. I'm sad that they got drafted to go to Vietnam, but I am a little relieved they are leaving me alone. Care for a smoke, Arthur?" Jimmy asked lighting one up.

"Oh, no Jimmy, somebody once told me those things will kill you," Arthur said playfully.

#

"To me, this world is nothing but evil, and my own evil just happened to come out cause of the circumstances of what I was doing.

-Aileen Wuornos; 7 victims; Rochester, Michigan USA

D r. Benson was running slightly late this morning. His graying and thinning hair was disheveled from the rush, and his brown trench coat was a convoluted array of fabric. While punctuality and order were his things, he lost track of time looking for his beloved Cornelius. He had left for his usual walkabout the night before and hadn't been back. It was highly unusual for him to be gone so long. He left often but was always back early to help Dr. Benson wake up.

"Good morning, Cathy," Dr. Benson said, shuffling in with an untidy look.

"Good morning, Dr. Benson. Everything okay?"

"Yes, just a crazy…just a busy morning." Dr. Benson caught himself using the word "crazy" out loud and quickly pulled back. Cathy, who was working the main security door at the entrance, had caught his faux pas and laughed out loud.

"Oh, Dr. Benson, you make me laugh you know that?"

"Why is that Cathy?"

"I think you're so serious. You should lighten up some. I mean you do manage the biggest hospital on the east coast. Have fun with it."

"You're right, Cathy. I'll try to do that today. I have an interesting session with an interesting fellow if you know what I mean," Dr. Benson said winking.

"There you go! You're getting it! Have a good day, Doctor."

"You too, Cathy."

Dr. Benson sat at his desk and looked at the clock. He had scheduled Arthur to come in first thing because he could hardly wait to hear more. He was fascinated and had spent most of the night thinking of Patrick. How could he get closer? How could he speak to him? All these things would help Dr. Benson achieve his goal he set when he first opened this place. His plans loomed big in front of his eyes. Today he would try to make that breakthrough.

"Dr. Benson, I have Arthur Fritz for you."

"Thank you, Gladys. Hello, Arthur. Take a seat. Relax."

"Good morning, Harold. Nice to see you again so quickly."

"Yes, well I thought deep last night about how to better help you. How to get through to you."

Arthur sat in the metal chair while Gladys moved the restraints.

"And what did you come up with, Harold?" Arthur asked.

"We have many options, Arthur. Many options," Dr. Benson said with a coy look while he waited for Gladys to leave the room.

A long pause brewed as Gladys did her thing and headed toward the door.

"Is Patrick here?" Dr. Benson asked.

"He's always here."

"I guess I don't have to tell you any more about me wanting to talk to Patrick.

"Why is that Harold? Why the hurry to speak with him?" Arthur asked.

"Well, Arthur…" Dr. Benson paused while he waited for the door to finally close. "Because you're sick. You're sick, and I need to get at the root of what is causing all of this. Patrick is not good for you, Arthur. He got you into this place. But you have the power to make him go away. I can help with that."

Arthur just stared blankly at Dr. Benson. It wasn't hard for him to pick up the sense of desperation in Dr. Benson's voice and body language. The less Arthur said, the more Dr. Benson pushed and poked, revealing his desires and plans.

"Is Patrick ready to talk?" Dr. Benson asked looking to the corner of the room.

"What are you looking at Harold?" Arthur asked.

"I'm looking at Patrick. You said he's here, right?"

"He is. But he's not over there."

"Well then, where is he?" Dr. Benson asked, moving his head around the room.

Arthur just smiled because he had the best view of Patrick out of anyone.

"He's standing right behind you, Harold."

Chills cascaded down Dr. Benson's neck and back. He had to remember that Arthur was sitting in front of him and Patrick was merely a fragment of Arthur's mind, but it gave Dr. Benson insight into where Arthur's thoughts were. For a second he felt that Patrick wanted to kill him, but in all his sovereignty, he couldn't foresee anything of the sort.

"What's he doing?"

"Nothing. He's just watching. But I have good news for you, Harold."

"And what might that be, Arthur?" Dr. Benson replied.

"Patrick said he's almost ready to meet you."

"That's great. I'm excited to talk to him as well."

"I have to caution you, Harold, Patrick can be...."

"Can be what?"

"Sometimes his intentions are not the best."

"I know that. Why do you think you're tied with chains to the chair?" Dr. Benson smiled and recovered his lost bravado, knowing that he was back in command.

"Arthur, tell me. What's your interest in Jimmy? I hear you've been talking to him quite a bit."

"I wouldn't say quite a bit, but yes, we have been getting to know him."

"And why him? There are other patients and staff around here."

"Yes, well, it's just who we gravitated toward, Harold. Listen, I'm feeling tired. Can we cut our session short?" Arthur said emphatically.

"But we are making progress, Arthur. Do you really want to stop now? Tell me more about Mr. Dale."

"I have nothing more to say about Mr. Dale. Nothing happened. Besides, I know it's Patrick you want to talk to, not me. So, I feel all of this is just a formality and waste of time until you can talk to him."

"That's true, but not entirely, Arthur. I honestly think Mr. Dale had something to do with your creation of Patrick."

"Mr. Dale is irrelevant. May I return to the rec room and hang out with George and Jimmy?

Dr. Benson moved forward in his chair a bit and repositioned his reading glasses.

"Yes, I suppose that's fine. But Patrick," Dr. Benson spoke as if there were actually a third person in the room, "you can't hide forever. Sooner or later you'll have to speak. And when you do, we are going to fix you up nice and good, you hear?"

Arthur didn't make a sound and Patrick just winked at Arthur. Things were starting to get interesting now.

****

April 26, 1967

The weather has been perfect. I've never cut so much wood in my life, but I'm about tired of it. I'm ready to get back to work. It's been over a month since Mrs. Denison was freed. A police officer came by asking me if I had seen or heard from Mrs. Denison. I told him the only thing I could—that her mind was slipping and she would wonder off sometimes. I told him she could be anywhere. He had no reason to suspect otherwise. After he left, I reminded myself that my calling was mine and mine alone. I often think back to the lion and remember that no one likes the lion, but nature made it for a reason. And that reason is healthy for the land. There is no need for justifying what I do because they can't see the big picture. They can't hear the souls, the way they talk to me. Their voices are beautiful, like that of angels or deities. And I sit here, merely a human. Who am I to defy what the gods want?

I feel that it is time again. It is time to do my job. I met a man yesterday in town. His name was Marvin Monte. He was a kind man, maybe in his late fifties. Everyone around him seemed to like him. I wish I had met him under different circumstances, we might have got along great. While Mr. Monte chatted up everyone in the grocery store, his soul spoke out to me in silence. He, too, was ready to be free of the flesh suit. He didn't even have to beg like Mrs. Denison. I told him I would help him out without questions. I made his soul aware that my actions and purpose are not exactly taken well by the populous. He understood my dilemma, and we worked out a plan for discretion. But in return for my services, I requested that I got to see his soul, not just hear it. He agreed. I often think back to when Mrs. Denison was freed. That tiny glimpse of her soul when I set it free. I know it might sound crazy, but it might have been the most beautiful and perfect thing I have ever seen. It glowed in a warm light that was welcoming, radiating peace and light. It took me a while, but I finally realized why I barely got a glimpse and not a full chance to bask in awe. I released her too quickly. My ax was fast and swift, but maybe it was too fast. While I told Arthur that our ways were flawed, he hesitated in knowing the pain it would cause, but he finally agreed to do things my way. Mr. Monte would not get the same treatment that Mrs. Denison got. No, he would have to endure much more. But like the zebra or gazelle, he will die with dignity and honor. While there is much pain, when it is over, there is none.

—Patrick

April 27, 1967

I have to admit I'm excited for Mr. Monte. Facing
death has never been more...rejuvenating. I saw
him again today. Not in person, but at a distance.
He lives in a rural area just outside of New Hope.
Nearly the exact opposite direction from where Mrs.
Denison and I lived. I studied his movements and
habits this afternoon. I observed he likes a girl
named Nancy. She seems to come over every
evening. She's not part of the equation at this
point, but she might be in the way of my meeting
with Mr. Monte. Today I feel odd, and I don't know
why. There's not much else to talk about today.

—Patrick

June 2, 1967

I've been getting up early and going to bed late,
but the fruits of my labor are ready to be shown
off. I now have, on the back end of my property, a
buried and fortified room. I've come to know it
affectionately as the Soul Laboratory. It's nearly
eight feet tall in there and exactly fifteen feet by
fifteen feet. Plenty of space to do what I need to do,
along with the privacy that I need to do it. With all
the paranoia over nuclear weapons being dropped, it
doubles as a bomb shelter too. I almost feel sorry
that Mrs. Denison didn't get the same great
treatment. Almost. I really would have loved to
have known her soul a little better. It just might be
the biggest regret in my life to date. I have to say
that it hasn't been all hard labor. I've been

observing Mr. Monte regularly. His habits amaze me. The patterns of all humans amaze me. The way they hang on to things, physical things as well as emotional. I understand because I, too, am just human. But am I? Along with my new duty, I feel...power. Like that of Zeus. I wonder if freeing the souls increases my power? I guess when Mr. Monte is released I'll find out. God, I love my job. It makes a difference in life when you love what you're doing. And right now, I've never been happier. It's almost time, Mr. Monte. I can hear you, and I'm making the proper preparations for your departure.

—Patrick

June 6, 1967

Mr. Monte is a fighter, a strong man who works hard on his farm. It's quite conflicting because the whole time his body put up a fight, his soul rejoiced in what was about to come. I had to block it out for a short while as I subdued Mr. Monte. But a good whack to the back of the head with a crowbar finally did the trick. I suspect he recognized me at first and was caught off guard. Indeed, he's a fighter, but my hard work on the Soul Lab has paid off. All that digging and concrete work has toughened me. Not to mention the fact that Mrs. Denison's soul has made me stronger. I feel like a young lion, making mistakes, but getting stronger and wiser as I go. I could best describe what's happening to me as a metamorphosis of sorts. Like that of a caterpillar. The change is never easy, and it's quite disgusting, to be honest. Just a few days ago, I saw a cocoon hanging on the porch behind my house. I took my pocket knife out and opened the cocoon for examination. Inside was a gooey mess of change. That glob of goop is a necessary step to get to the beauty of a butterfly. I am that mess right now.

The Soul Lab is equipped with restraints built into the walls and a table in the middle. It, too, has restraints hanging off the edge. While the body doesn't want it, the soul quietly and calmly waits. It's the only reason I could do what I do. Otherwise, I'd likely be labeled a crazy. Mr. Monte fit perfectly onto the table and awoke just shortly after I strapped him in. He asked why I was doing this and where he was. I listened to his questions but ultimately decided that talking to him and trying to tell him my purpose was a waste of time. A mere human wouldn't understand the complex mission I'm on. He just wouldn't. So, while he begged and pleaded for conversation, I simply ignored him and instead listened to the dulcet and angelic tones of the soul. I was eager to meet him. The real him. The anticipation was building, and I could hardly take it, but I had to take my time. I didn't get to know Mrs. Denison's soul the way I wanted to. I wouldn't make the same mistake with Mr. Monte. He deserved better. They all did.

Mr. Monte's hand wiggled in the straps like a five-year-old that couldn't keep still. I studied his hands and saw how rough they were. He had worked hard his whole life. He contributed to this country a great deal. It's a shame his soul was ready to go. And I ask again, who am I to upset the gods? Mr. Monte spoke with such conviction about how I "don't have to do this" and he "didn't do anything to me." I felt like that was the appropriate time to engage in conversation with him.

Poor Mr. Monte looked at me and barely had a reaction after I told him why. Just as I predicted, he couldn't understand. It was a complete waste to tell him, it fell on deaf ears. The only reaction he had was his eyes growing wide when I told him I was setting his soul free and how I would do it…slowly. That's when his reaction changed drastically.

I took a break from the yelling and screaming for a second to run back into the house. A great artist always had their tools in order. This time I had made somewhat of an investment into my trade with the purchase of some medical grade surgical equipment. It's amazing what you can order through the mail these days. They sell just about anything through catalogs. It makes my job wonderfully easy. They arrived a few days ago, and I took the liberty of making a leather scabbard for all the tools. I inspected each one and cleaned them. Boy, stainless steel is a thing of beauty. I like to stare into the blade of the large scalpel and see my reflection. It's slightly distorted. Perhaps it is an accurate representation of myself. When I look in the mirror, I see the same distortion. Which one is real? It's hard to tell anymore.

—Patrick

NINE

"I like killing people because it is so much fun. It is more fun than killing wild game in the forest because man is the most dangerous animal of them all."

-Zodiac Killer; 7-37 victims; Location unknown

June 7, 1967

Mr. Monte and I both have rested well through the night. Even though it's sunny and warm outside, Mr. Monte was comfortable in the bunker in the well-regulated, sixty-five-degree room. I awoke with vigor this morning. Days like today are the reason for my being. How can I not be excited? I made a pot of coffee on the wood-burning stove. I take it black. I find I get the most out of it that way. I find I'm closer to the bean. I'm closer to the original form. Just like Mr. Monte.

A couple of fried eggs with dry toast, that's a good breakfast for me. Was the coffee too strong or am I just that excited? The butterflies in my stomach must have drank some of that coffee. I climbed into the bunker through some basic wooden steps made from two-by-eight studs. Sturdy really. Mr. Monte had worked himself into a frenzy it seemed.

His wrists were rubbed raw from trying to escape. If he only knew the good I was doing.

I'm accustomed to hearing curse words, though I rarely use them. I think last time I cursed was when I got a pretty good-sized splinter in my finger and it hurt like hell. But Mr. Monte is downright pissed! He's using words I would never dare say. No matter the hatred coming from him, I remained calm. I'm performing a service, something no one else wants to do. I am the lion. Everyone wants to be the lion, but nobody wants to kill the zebra. I have to remind myself of that often. No more messing around. Time to be the lion. I used my pocket knife to cut off Mr. Monte's shirt. I instantly regretted doing that. It was a fairly good shirt. Mr. Monte was just about the same size as me. To correct my mistake, I eyed his work boots. Red Wings. What a find. Those are good boots. After the release, I'll definitely be keeping those.

With his bare chest showing on the wooden table, I unfolded my new tools gently. Mr. Monte went quickly from hating me to begging me to let him go. I told him that that is precisely what I'm doing. The look on his face told me he didn't get it. I pulled my little table that my tools sat on over next to the big table. Time to earn my keep. I wanted to meet him so badly and the time was finally here. As I grabbed the big scalpel and held it in the air, Mr. Monte's eyes dilated as large as pennies.

It is amazing how soft and fragile the human body is. I took a large square, probably twelve square inches off his left pectoral muscle. The sharp blade made easy work of his skin and muscle. I peeled it back easily, and only his breastplate was left showing. I shushed Mr. Monte when the screaming nearly got unbearable. But I quickly remembered what he was going through. It was perfectly acceptable for the gazelle and zebra to bray out. The only words I ever spoke out during his release were "It's okay to yell, Mr. Monte. Nobody can hear you down here". Was I laughing when I said that?? Now that only the bone remained, I took out the small hand saw that would go through bone like butter. My overall objective was to get the heart. The heart is the life of the body. And there is where I believed I would see the soul escape. I took a moment to look Mr. Monte in the eyes. Sweat and tears ran down his face. I could see the pain, but I assured him it would be okay and that I was nearly done. As painful as the removal of the flesh was, the sawing through the bone with no anesthesia could only be described as unbearable. Adding to that, the thick concrete walls echoed the screams of Mr. Monte back into my ears. This is why the job belongs to me. I sawed vigorously through his breastplate and sternum. I had to be careful. All that bone was there to protect the heart. I made sure none of my sawing would accidentally puncture or hit the heart. The human body is remarkable, but no match for surgical-grade stainless steel. After it was all said and done, we were both sweating. The only difference now was Mr. Monte had stopped screaming. I can

only guess he finally went into shock. His face
was a ghostly ash color in the pale light provided
from the overhead bulb. The only thing I didn't
account for was all the blood. I used a towel from
the house to sop it up, but it made little difference.
Maybe I should have cauterized it with some sort of
heating iron. I'll have to remember that for next
time. I wiped the sweat from my head, and I was at
my moment. There was Mr. Monte's beating heart
for all the world to see.

It had tremendous strength to it. What a muscle. It
powered the whole body. That little object was
responsible for building the pyramids. But also,
making nuclear weapons. So many things of awe
but also so many things of destruction. Mr.
Monte's eyes followed my eyes. He couldn't
imagine what would come next…but I knew. I
gingerly leaned over to my tool table and took the
small, but agile scalpel out. I had to work quickly
now, Mr. Monte was starting to fade. I was about
to take his heart and set free his soul. The soft
arteries and veins of Mr. Monte were no match
against the razor-sharp blade. In two seconds, I
held Mr. Monte's beating heart in my hand.
Incredible how long it took to finally stop. And,
finally, the reason for all of this…his soul. It left
the heart in what I thought was slow motion. I
wasn't let down. Oh, my…how awe-inspiring it
was. It started out as a very fine mist. At first, I
thought it would pass me by, but then it appeared
in its full form. I wish I had the words to describe
it. Hearing and talking to the soul was one thing,
seeing it was another altogether. Once again it

thanked me for my help. It was so gracious in doing so. Just when I thought it was leaving, it became a part of me, just as I had hoped. And in an instant, my power surged to a new level. By the time the heart stopped pulsing in my hand, Mr. Monte's eyes were rolled back into his head. He had endured so much. I was proud of him.

Arthur couldn't have handled this one. But like a good assistant, he was there to clean up after. Disposal of the flesh was where Arthur excelled the most. I couldn't tell you what he did with the bodies.

I feel fantastic. I don't even know where to start. I'm more powerful and wiser than I've ever been. To find one's calling is to fulfill the destiny that the universe has set forth. I'm a young lion...I'm not going anywhere. But for now, I need my rest. It's time for reflection and respite. I've done well, and there are many zebras left...

—Patrick

★★★★★★★★★★

Every time Dr. Benson thought of meeting with Arthur, he became a duplication of Pavlov's dog, salivating at the thought about the books he would write; the lectures he would be giving at prestigious colleges and universities. His plan to make Arthur his meal ticket was starting to come alive. What he didn't know was that the same thing for Arthur and Patrick was true. Although he was an in-control and well-educated man, there were many, many things Dr. Benson didn't know.

"Come in!" Dr. Benson shouted from one of his file cabinets.

"Hello, Dr. Benson," Gladys said.

"Hi. What is it, Gladys?"

"Well, there's an issue we have going on. Jimmy hasn't been to work for three whole days. He's not missed a single day since he's been here, so, I'm a lil' worried," she said in her southern voice. "I called his parents yesterday. They haven't heard from him. They found it unusual to not hear from him either. I haven't gone to his apartment yet."

"Okay. Why don't you take one of the cars, go into town and drop by his place? Maybe he's sick or something. I'll call the police and see what they can do."

"Dr. Benson?" Gladys had a profound look of concern on her face. She nearly looked terrified.

"Yes, Gladys?"

"I have a bad feeling about this, Dr. Benson. I mean…"

The usually confident and strong Gladys suddenly looked a little shook up. She was the rock around these parts. She was Dr. Benson's right hand. It was a little unnerving to see her like this.

"What's wrong, Gladys?"

"He's been talking to Arthur quite a bit lately. I think he was star struck with him."

"Gladys, I know what you're thinking, but Arthur is here. He's in our care. He's not going to hurt anyone anymore."

"Maybe, but I just have a bad feeling Doctor."

"I know he's a scary man, Gladys, but you have to be careful not to show that fear around the staff. They look to you as their leader. You have got to be strong. Can you handle that?"

A warm feeling came back over Gladys.

"Thank you, Dr. Benson. You are right. I'm sorry. It's just…"

"I know, Gladys. I'm well aware of what he's done, trust me. And he has a very agreeable demeanor about him. It's eerie, I know."

"I'm good now, Dr. Benson. I'm sorry for that," Gladys said, regaining her composure.

"It's okay, Gladys. Arthur is a once-in-a-lifetime patient. We will be writing books about him for years to come. But our protocol is in place for a reason. Don't worry."

"Thank you again, Doctor. I'll send someone out to Jimmy's apartment immediately."

"Good day, Gladys."

Dr. Benson shuffled some files around his desk and worked on updating Arthur's file, mostly documenting the few discussions that had already taken place. Gladys hadn't been gone more than five minutes before she was back again. The first time she arrived she had a look of fear and dread on her face. When she left, she had her confidence back. After not more than five minutes, the first look was back again.

"Please, come in," Dr. Benson said to the stranger with Gladys.

The man removed his brown fedora hat before crossing the threshold into Dr. Benson's office. His matted dark hair matched his jacket perfectly with the same shade of black. His heavy leather jacket seemed to weight him down, but it was necessary with the cold air coming down from the north. Dr. Benson stood and tightened his white lab coat while extending his right hand.

"Hello. I'm Dr. Benson. I usually only see people by appointments. What's this about?"

The man returned the handshake and casually took off his coat while making himself at home by taking a seat.

"My name is Detective Reynolds. I'm here to ask you some questions about a James Barnett."

"Oh yes, Jimmy. Is everything alright?" Dr. Benson asked.

"Not exactly. We found his body last night. I need to ask you a few questions."

It didn't take long for Dr. Benson to wear the same look on his face as Gladys…

TEN

"I didn't want to hurt them, I only wanted to kill them."

-David Berkowitz "Son of Sam"; 6 victims; Brooklyn, New York USA

D r. Benson didn't know how to react other than to look down and stare at his feet for a second.

"I don't know what to say. I mean, he was missing for the last few days. In fact, I just sent someone over to his house to check in on him. What happened?"

"I'm afraid it's more serious than just what happened to him. The Chief of Police and Mayor Jenkins are in a frenzy over this one."

"Over Jimmy? Why?"

"Since the court has remanded Arthur Fritz to your hospital, has he left your sight or this facility?"

A tingle ran down Dr. Benson's back. He was starting to feel the control he loved so much slipping away.

"Why Detective! Of course he's not left. What kind of hospital do you think I run?"

"Well, I have to ask these questions, Dr. Benson. You see, the Mayor and Chief of Police are concerned because Jimmy was murdered. He was killed in the same fashion as some of the victims of Arthur Fritz."

Dr. Benson was speechless, but he wasn't about to start thinking that he had a problem with Arthur leaving the facility.

"What about a copycat killer?" Dr. Benson asked.

"Doctor, please let me solve the cases, and you treat your patients."

"I wasn't trying to…"

"We considered that, but the details of the murder…well, let's just say that if it isn't Arthur Fritz, then we got a world full of sick bastards running around. Makes me want to hole up in a cave somewhere far away from people.

Dr. Benson could tell by looking at Detective Reynolds that what he saw had shaken him up.

"Did you work any of the other murders on Arthur Fritz?" Dr. Benson asked.

"I helped some, but I never saw any of the victims in the field. I only saw pictures, which were bad enough. I did, however, arrest him. Do you mind if I smoke?"

"Not at all. Please. We may have gotten off on the wrong foot, but we need to work together. I will do anything in my power to help you."

Detective Reynolds pulled a Belair menthol cigarette from his inside jacket pocket and flicked his Zippo lighter open.

"When Jimmy, as you call him, was reported missing, I was put on the case. That same day we got a call from an apartment supervisor about a strange odor coming from Jimmy's apartment. It was enough to get a warrant and break down the door. Now, Doctor, I'm sure you might be used to seeing such things in your profession, and I should be too, but this isn't the kind of town where those things happen. I had no idea what to expect when we broke the door down, but what I saw will haunt me the rest of my life."

Just listening to Detective Reynolds tell the story and with the fear you could see in his eyes, Dr. Benson was starting to understand. The police files were bad enough, now to hear the stories from a shaken-up cop was even more disturbing.

"Can you tell me what you saw?"

"Are you sure you want to know?" Detective Reynolds asked him back.

"Well if I'm to help you in any way I think it's better that I do, wouldn't you agree?"

Detective Reynolds took a long drag in from the halfway burnt cigarette and blew out a big plume of smoke as if to exhale stress along with the smoke.

"Look, Dr. Benson. I'm a strong man. In fact, I feel a little bad showing you the least bit of fear. To see a man, to see a man in that condition. Anyway, I was the first in the door, and the smell was pretty bad. The heater was left on high, and I think that allowed the body to rot something good."

Dr. Benson moved slightly closer in like a man captivated by a movie or story.

"Under normal circumstances, I wouldn't be able to tell you these kinds of details, but the mayor okayed it. So please, keep this stuff to yourself," Detective Reynolds said with stiff eyebrows.

"Jimmy was tied up to a chair with his arms behind him. He was completely naked. His right leg was skinned. And by skinned, I mean skinned, like you would a deer. Next to him was a bucket full of blood and a tube coming out of his leg. Now it took some time to figure it out, but Jimmy had a small incision on his lower back. The conclusion we came to was that whoever did this, severed Jimmy's spinal cord, making him feel nothing below that. He then skinned the leg to find the femoral artery. That tube coming out of his leg…that was the artery. The bastard cut it and bled poor Jimmy out into that bucket." Detective Reynolds dropped his head and paused for a second. "What kind of sick son of a bitch does something like that?"

Dr. Benson didn't have an answer for him. But if he did, it would be Arthur Fritz.

"I mean there were chunks of meat and a pile of skin…goddammit."

Dr. Benson looked to be the rock on the outside, but on the inside, he could only wonder if it was Arthur. But it couldn't be. He was safe inside the confines of New Hope Psychiatric Hospital.

"Well, Detective, let me tell you, I run a tight operation here. I can assure you without any hesitation that Arthur is in our care and he hasn't gotten out. I literally built this facility from the ground up. I oversaw all of it, every phase of construction. If you'd like, I can run you down to see his cell. Would that make you feel better?" Dr. Benson asked.

"No. That's okay, doctor. I had to come and ask you know?"

"Yes. I understand just fine."

"Do you know or can you think of anyone who would want to hurt Jimmy?"

"Not one bit. He was a gentle kid. He was excited to work here. I can't imagine anyone doing that to him. I can only imagine that Arthur has some very disturbed fans out there who might be trying to carry on his legacy."

"Yeah, that's what I think, too."

Detective Reynolds stood up, put his jacket back on, and gently laid his fedora back on his head.

"I might need to interview some of your other staff if that's okay?"

"Sure. Gladys will show you around, and you can talk to anyone you need to. Listen, I'm going to leave you the number here to my office. If anything comes up, please let me know."

"Thank you. And here's my number. On that same note, if you think of anything or come across any information, please let me know. The Chief's hair is on fire with this. We have got to put it out. The last thing this little town needs is another Arthur Fritz."

"I couldn't agree with you more, Detective. Have a good day."

"You too, Dr. Benson."

"Gladys?" Dr. Benson asked through the phone.

"Yes, Dr. Benson?"

"I've cleaned off my schedule for the afternoon. Get Arthur up here after lunch, will you?"

"Certainly, Dr. Benson. Is everything all right?"

"Yes, it's fine. Detective Reynolds will fill you in on what happened to Jimmy."

"He already told me. Remember that feeling I had? I told you. My grandma had that power too. When she sensed sometin' wasn't right, she knew it. And I did too."

"I know, Gladys. But everything is going to be all right, you hear me?"

"I understand you, Dr. Benson, but I don't know if I believe you."

★★★★★★★★★★

"Good afternoon, Harold!" Arthur shouted.

"Hello, Arthur. You seem to be in a good mood today. I think those meds are working great for you."

"Well, maybe. But I just had a fine lunch with George. That guy sure is a lively fella."

"Yes, he is. Please sit down. Gladys, will you kindly shackle Mr. Fritz for me? Thank you."

Dr. Benson appeared to be a little more nervous than he normally was. Patrick picked up on it immediately. Gladys put the keys back in her pocket and slowly closed the door. Being near Arthur suddenly gave her the creeps.

"So, I didn't think we had a session today, Harold. What's going on?"

"Well, I just wanted to talk, Arthur. The more time I get with you, the more I get to help."

"Great. Well, let's go then."

Arthur stretched his fingers as if getting ready for a fight.

"Tell me about you and Jimmy?"

"What would you like to know? I haven't seen him in a few days."

"Gladys tells me you guys talk a lot. What do you two talk about?"

Arthur didn't seem rattled by the question nor did he appear to know anything was wrong.

"You know, mostly about his time on the farm and his brothers. Nothing too serious."

"I see. Anything else of note?"

"Can't say there is. He's a good kid. I like him. I wish I could say the same for Patrick."

Dr. Benson perked up in his chair upon hearing the name.

"What makes you say that?"

"Well, Patrick thinks he is weak. He said Jimmy is slowing the herd down."

"What herd?"

"Humanity."

"Did he tell you this?"

"Patrick is getting close to meeting with you. Until then, I can only speculate what's going on inside his head. But soon, Harold." Arthur said with a sarcastic undertone.

"I want to change the topic here. I do eventually want to speak with him, but right now I want to know more about you. Tell me about what you did before, well, before the things that got you into this place."

"They always told me I was smart and good at building things. I didn't have much use for school. I barely finished the twelfth grade. Not because it was too hard, but because I was bored. Biology was my favorite class. Always captured my interest. You must know a thing or two about biology, right Harold?"

"Yes, I have taken a class or two in that. Of course, I'm being facetious. But please, tell me what piqued your interest in biology?"

"It's amazing. All life forms seem to be little machines with the same programming."

"And what programming might that be?"

"To survive, Harold. At any cost. Take viruses for example. They go to the point of survival so much that they even kill their own host."

"And how is that good for them in that case?"

"Because Harold. They are extremely contagious and incredibly selfless. They die so that the virus, or the greater good, can live on. They also morph to adapt to their environment. And they can survive, kind of like humans. We are a virus. We are destroying our own host, and we know it, but it's like we're powerless to stop it. Look at the bombs we've built. Look at the wars we fight. One big virus, Harold."

Dr. Benson scribbled some notes down on his pad and looked back up at Arthur. "So, is this why you believe in what Patrick is doing?"

"I guess so."

A long and awkward pause finally broke when Dr. Benson found his next question. "So, they said you were good at building? What did you get into next then?"

"What else but construction?"

Dr. Benson let out a slight chuckle.

"Is that funny Harold?" Arthur said slightly annoyed.

"No, it's just ironic. Because you are all about destruction, not construction."

"Harold, is this how you treat all your patients?"

"What do you mean?"

"With condescension and arrogance? Oh no, usually just drugs and brain scrambles, eh?"

"Oh, Arthur, did I strike a nerve?"

Arthur stared blankly at Dr. Benson. Dr. Benson's control was slipping, and the only way to get it back was beat up on the soft and unusually calm Arthur.

"No, Harold, you didn't. It did hurt my feelings, but I'm okay."

"Well, I can't say I'm sorry if this hurts your feelings, Arthur, but the truth is, you are a deranged criminal who has been found criminally insane and responsible for multiple brutal murders. That's the truth. And let me give you another truth while we're here. Jimmy, your friend? He's been found murdered in the same nasty fashion that you're accustomed to."

"I told you. It was Patrick."

"You say that Arthur, but Patrick isn't here, is he? Just you. Bring him on out. Let's talk with him!"

"I've told you many times, Harold. He's not ready. But I warn you to be careful what you wish for. He's brilliant, and he's very tactful."

Dr. Benson chuckled. The chipper mood that once occupied Arthur was gone. Dr. Benson managed to take him down a peg. The slight perception of the control of his facility slipping made him need to feel that he was still the boss. Verbally beating up on Arthur brought him right back to feeling okay.

"Oh, and I'm sorry about Jimmy," Arthur said in a lowly tone.

"Our session is over now, Arthur. Gladys will take you back to the common area."

"Goodbye, Harold."

"Goodbye, Arthur."

ELEVEN

"Every man to his own tastes. Mine is to corpses."

-Henri Blot; Unknown number of victims; France

August 14, 1967

Where did summer go? Looking back now, it was a whirlwind of fun. Mostly learning about myself, but fun nonetheless. I can honestly say that I've taken huge steps in my development. I see things more clearly. It's like the speed of the world has slowed down for me. The clarity...it's remarkable. For example, yesterday I had the most eloquent conversation with a doe in the trees. I was out scouting for deer for the hunt next week when I stumbled upon her. Like a good prey, she saw me before I saw her. Then we just stared at each other for the longest time. Finally, I broke the silence by saying hello and that I will be on the hunt in a few weeks and she should probably go away. But what she said completely took me by surprise, and it made me think. She asked why the fight was so lopsided. I didn't know what she meant, but as I inquired further, she reminded me that I have a gun with a scope on it. All she had was great hearing and a little camouflage. She took off quickly after that. I got the feeling she didn't like me too much. But I started to think...maybe she's right. I'm the lion. Why do I only pick on the weak and sick? I know it's the way nature works, but what if I want a challenge? Mrs. Denison wasn't a challenge, and Mr. Monte was too easy. I'm going to have to give this some serious thought.

—Patrick.

August 28, 1967

I met an old soul today, and it just fascinated me. An old drifter from the West Coast. His name is Miles Worther. He's a young fella, maybe in his late twenties. I was driving into town in the old pickup, and there he was on the side of the road with his thumb in the air. I asked him where he was going. He said anywhere but where he was. Man, Miles loves to talk. He can tell stories too. It seems Miles had joined the hippie movement back west and ended up doing all sorts of drugs. Drugs and women, he said. I asked him if it was so good, then why did he leave? He told me that it seemed like the thing to do, but nobody was serious about anything. All they did was talk big and dream big. I told him "welcome to the ways of the world, friend." We got along well, so I invited him to stay with me. The guest bedroom was clean and all set up. He didn't have much stuff, and he had nowhere to go. It was a natural choice for him.

—Patrick

August 29, 1967

Day 1 of having Miles in the house. I've always lived alone, and it was sort of a weird feeling to have someone in the house at night and in the morning. But I'll get along just fine. Arthur is adjusting as well, but he's a people person, so no surprise there. Miles has pretty much kept to himself, and Arthur's been doing what Arthur does. This morning for breakfast I made Miles and me some fresh eggs from the chicken coop. It sounds weird, but I think Miles thought that eggs came from the supermarket. He was that far gone on drugs and the belief that the working system was a farce or it was just "the man" that was out to get him. It became evident that he didn't know a hard day's work in his life. I'm sure his parents were hard-working Americans, and he was just rebelling. Maybe out here he'll learn the value of work. This afternoon I'm going to introduce Miles to the woodpile and my ax.

—Patrick

August 30, 1967

Miles spoke to me today. From the inside. It was beautiful, like an angel singing to me. I don't know if it was me watching him swing that ax or the cold fall air, but something brought his soul out to talk. He told me he was tired. Tired of all the drugs Miles had done, and the damage to his physical body was beyond repair. He said some egos just abuse the body, and the soul is what has to take the ultimate punishment. I like Miles, but I like my job more. And I love meeting the souls above anything else. Oh, well, he was such a fresh guy. I'll miss him. Of all the souls I've talked to, this is the one I'm most enamored with...not sure why. Maybe the deer put some thoughts into my head that got me thinking. Maybe Miles is a better prey than the others. Either way, I'll enjoy this one.

—Patrick

September 3, 1967

Miles was packing his bags in the bedroom, and I had to wash up before showing him where his fate lies. I took a good long look in the mirror. I've grown. I've changed, and the transformation is nothing less than a miracle. The timid and sheepish man that I once was is now replaced by a smart and capable man who will bring about a change in this world. The kind of change that the gods would be proud of. I love who I'm becoming.

Miles wants to leave in the morning. I can't let that happen because I know what needs to be done. Time to punch that time card, as they say. I had shown him most of the property except for my little dugout. It was about the right time for him to see it. I have a special treatment I've been saving up for Miles. It will cause him more pain than any human should have to experience, but the release of his soul will be magical.

Miles thought I might make and store wine in the cellar. It didn't take long before he knew that the cellar wasn't for making wine. I struck him in the back with a shovel, and when he fell to his knees in shock, I placed the chloroform rag over his mouth. It quickly did its thing, and the struggle was over. I stripped Miles and chained him to the wall. He wasn't the biggest on personal hygiene, so I hosed him off until he finally snapped out of his sleep. The bewildered look on his face was worth a million dollars. They always started off so confused. They don't understand how important the work is I'm doing. And when I try to explain it to them they look at me like I'm crazy. That look can be a bit frustrating.

—Patrick

September 4, 1967

The day has arrived. It's going to take longer than a day, but today is the day we start. My friend Miles is now begging and pleading, which somehow amuses me. I think it amuses me because I'm only doing what their inner being desires. My reward is getting to meet that soul. To see a soul in person…we would all endure such things if we only knew how beautiful it was. Maybe, one day, my soul will ask to be let go. I'll understand that logic knowing what I know now. But until that day, it's my job to help other souls. I wonder if there are others out there like me? I'm certain there must be. Oh, well, onward and upward we go!

I've been planning this release for a while. A few months ago, while walking through the trees, I came across the carcass of a wolf. It didn't smell too bad. In fact, there was hardly any meat on it. I could tell it was an older animal...the teeth were worn down. He was a good-sized wolf, too. I could see maggots eating what little was left of the meat, and it got me to thinking how efficient nature is. These bones were picked clean except for a few spots. I imagine the soul will leak and ease out of the body in this type of fashion, so I grabbed a handful of bones and put them in the foil that I had my sandwich in. Later that afternoon, I went to the local library and did some reading on maggots. I was surprised to learn that they are used on gangrene and burn victims as they only eat dead flesh. They won't touch it if it's still alive. This is going to be fun.

Miles wasn't in that high of spirits, especially after I told him what was going to happen to him. He screamed uncontrollably and sobbed like a child.

—Patrick

September 7, 1967

Poor Miles. He has no idea what kind of pain he's in for. I put a deep cut on both of his feet a few days back. I allowed them to get infected, and the smell is proof that he is indeed rotting away. I put a tourniquet just above his ankles, so he gets little blood flow. His feet are nearly black, and I'm confident they are rotting. Miles has a decent fever going on as the infection is spreading. But this morning I introduced the maggots. Man, are they hungry! I put them on and released the tourniquet so the infection would move up his leg, providing more food for the little guys to chomp on. I asked Miles what it felt like. He only cursed and called me crazy. I'll see what he looks like in the morning.

—Patrick

September 8, 1967

Oh, those magnificent little creatures have done well! I can see his ankle bone starting to come out through the rotten meat. I've provided Miles with some food and water to help keep his strength up. He pushed it away at first, but now he's eating something. Pride is never stronger than the need to stay alive. He's running a fever too. I pray his body stays strong for a little while longer. I love to hear him beg about how he won't go to the authorities. I replied by telling him I know he won't because he'll be dead after this. I couldn't help but laugh hysterically at the look on his face when I said that. Priceless.

I put some more cuts on his upper leg. They could become infected quickly. Oh, and I also learned that maggots come from flies. It's getting chilly up here, but we still have plenty. I trapped some in the house and introduced them to the new cuts. There will be plenty of maggots to complete the task. I tell you one thing, I've never had so much fun in my life as I am right now. Am I crazy? I don't think so. Miles might disagree.

—Patrick

September 11, 1967

Miles is barely hanging in there. He's alive, but I'm not sure for how much longer. I've given him an IV bag, and that seems to be helping. He only mumbles now. Maybe his pride finally did step aside to let himself die. I expected more of a fight, but then again, he's simply outmatched. I must say the human body is remarkable. The maggots have gotten nearly above his knees. Nothing but bone and tendons. And when I say bone, I mean white, shiny bone, picked clean. Just like the wolf I saw. Amazing. I imagine Miles is in shock, but as soon as they work their way up, it'll be the end of the line for him. He's not even talking to me anymore. As least Arthur will know what to do with the body.

—Patrick

September 12, 1967

Something isn't right. I don't feel the same.

—Patrick

September 13, 1967

It appears Miles didn't make it through the night. But what a sight his body is! A skeleton on the bottom, a regular torso up top. I'd like to pretend I saw his soul escaping, but let's be real. We have no souls. At least I don't. My hunger and lust for death have subsided for now. We'll see how long before it rears its ugly head again.

—Patrick

September 14, 1967

Change is brewing inside. Like the calm before the storm. I vividly remember I could see the souls when I was what you would call normal, I guess. Now...now I've risen above. I used to think my job was a part of nature. I used to think I had a purpose, but all of that has changed now. The souls, hardly there. I think I may have made them up. So, what is it?

—Patrick

September 15, 1967

It came to me in a dream last night. Clear as day. There's no other way around it. I can't dispute what's happening to me. I'm no longer doing this because I feel I have to, I'm doing

this because I like it. No, I don't even like it.
I'm lying again. I love it...

—Patrick

TWELVE

"Even when she was dead, she was still bitching at me. I couldn't get her to shut up!"

-Edmund Kemper; 6 victims; Burbank, California USA

"Detective Reynolds?" Dr. Benson asked.

"Yes, who is this?"

"This is Dr. Benson over at New Hope Psychiatric Hospital."

"Oh, hey, Dr. Benson. How are you?" Detective Reynolds replied in a calm voice.

"I'm doing well. Can't say that our staff isn't a little shook up."

"Yeah, I hear you. New Hope's guard is back up. There is just no convincing people that Arthur Fritz is locked away and that he didn't kill Jimmy. But I can understand their fears."

"I was calling to see if you had made any progress on the case?"

"As of now, no. We are basically doing damage control to keep this thing as quiet as possible. I just hope nobody else gets killed, or we might have panic in the streets over this. People are scared, you know?" Detective Reynolds said, rudely chewing food while on the phone.

"As they should be. I remember when they caught Arthur, it was like the entire town took a collective sigh and dropped their pitchforks."

"Well, thanks for calling, Dr. Benson, I appreciate it."

"No problem, Reynolds. Oh, and give the Mayor my regards."

"I will."

Dr. Benson and Mayor Don Jenkins went back a long way. Don was a key figure in convincing the city council to put up half the funding to build New Hope Psychiatric Hospital. Dr. Benson wondered why he hadn't heard from Mayor Jenkins sooner on this matter. Dr. Benson chalked it up to him being busy with things that mayors have to do.

The evening had come quickly, and Dr. Benson had just seen his last patient. He made a habit of bringing his jacket due to the chilly mornings they'd been having over the last few weeks. He slung it over his shoulder, turned off the lamp on his desk and headed down the stairs to his right. It was already dark outside, and the red light to hell was well lit.

"Late night, Dr. Benson?" the security guard asked.

"Yes, it is, Charlie. You know how that goes."

"I most certainly do, Sir! Have a good night, Dr. Benson."

"You too, Charlie."

Dr. Benson was nearly through the door when he stopped in his tracks. Charlie stood still at the check-in counter and noticed the hesitation.

"Everything okay, Dr. Benson?"

"Yes, Charlie. I just think I forgot to check on something."

He did an about face and quickly scurried past the desk and down the hallway to the first security gate.

"Buzz me in, Charlie, will ya?"

"You got it, Sir!" Charlie yelled back.

Doubt had been slowly creeping into the brain of the good doctor over the last few weeks, and this was his place. He would restore that doubt by confirming his authority in these walls. His patent leather shoes squeaked against the perfectly uniform and repeating tile squares. All the cell doors were locked tightly, and the lights dimmed for effect. If Dr. Benson hadn't been so used to it, he would have been frightened to be walking inches from the most deranged criminals on the east coast. Not to mention the infamous Arthur Fritz, whose cell he was fast approaching on his left. The echoes of his footsteps slowly came to a halt as he finally reached the door. In the center of it was a small porthole of sorts with metal wire embedded in between the panels of shatterproof glass. Without wanting to cast too much of a shadow into the room, he slowly moved his head in front of the window. There he was, the sickest serial killer almost anyone had ever heard of, just sitting at a desk with the light off, staring at a piece of paper. But nothing got by Arthur. He slowly turned his head to the right, and his eyes met Dr. Benson's. Dr. Benson stood stoic with a half-cocked smile on his face.

"I'm still in charge here, asshole," Dr. Benson muttered under his breath.

Arthur just smiled right back at him.

"Arthur, does he understand what he's signed up for?" Patrick asked.

"I'm not sure if he does, Patrick. I'm not sure if he does."

★★★★★★★★★★

Dr. Benson's house would have been completely pitch black if not for the small hallway light he left on for Cornelius. Even though he could see in the dark, it gave him some comfort in knowing his little fellow wasn't totally in the blackness.

"Cornelius!" Dr. Benson yelled into the living room.

A tiny and faint meow could be heard coming from the kitchen as Dr. Benson hung his coat on the hook behind the door.

"There he is! There's the man of the house."

Cornelius circled and rubbed up on the leg of his master at the same time Dr. Benson kneeled and gently scratched his friend's soft coat.

"What did you do today Mr. Cornelius?" Only a big meow ensued, but Dr. Benson surely knew what that meant.

"Oh, I know. Come on, let's go in the kitchen, and I'll make you something to eat."

It was nearly eleven p.m. on Friday, but long and late nights were nothing new to Dr. Benson. He was used to working late and often long hours, which is maybe why he chose a cat over a dog.

"Alright, Mr. C., I think I need a shower, and then we can put this day behind us. What do you say? Tomorrow we can go outside and tidy up the yard and house for winter. Sound good?"

Instead of letting out his trademark meow, Cornelius just followed Dr. Benson down the lit hallway and into the bedroom. The tiny bathroom was adjoined to the master bedroom. On the opposite side of the house was a small extra bedroom that Dr. Benson converted into a study so he could do research. Overall, it was a decent little house right on the outskirts of New Hope where the more affluent live.

Dr. Benson turned the knob to the hot water, and a cloud of steam rose from the cold porcelain. He stripped down, and before he could take off his last sock, the tiny bathroom was filled with steam. Cornelius just sat on the toilet and licked the inside of his left front leg. Dr. Benson hummed a song he had heard on the radio by a group called The Beatles. In between the offbeat hums, Dr. Benson could only think of dead Jimmy, Detective Reynolds, the Mayor up in arms, and Arthur Fritz, sitting in his cell. Dr. Benson's smug sense of control awarded him a small sense of victory. Dr. Benson was winning the battle, but he was about to lose the war...

"What do you have to say about my singing Mr. C.?" Dr. Benson belted out as the last drop of water from the showerhead hit the tub.

Grabbing a towel from the towel rack and peeking at the floor, he couldn't help noticing that Cornelius was gone and the door to the bathroom was cracked.

"Hmm. I could have sworn I shut the door. Do you have opposable thumbs Mr. C.?"

Still no response. Dr. Benson grabbed the towel and began to pat himself dry as he yanked open the shower curtain to get a view of where Cornelius ran off to. With the combination of not having his glasses on and being distracted by the whereabouts of Cornelius, Dr. Benson didn't notice the writing on the fog of the mirror. Stepping out and grabbing his glasses from the sink, it was right there in his blurred reflection, mocking him, knowing his inner secrets.

Who is Tommy B.?

"Cornelius!?" Dr. Benson shouted with a slightly higher pitched voice than normal.

There he stood, motionless in the misty bathroom, like prey that knows it's being stalked in a sweaty jungle. With his ears fully tuned in, he finally heard a noise, a familiar meow from Cornelius, who acted as if Dr. Benson had just got home.

"Are you okay?" Dr. Benson asked.

He didn't know if he was asking the cat or himself. He was sure about Cornelius, but not so much himself. Someone was just feet away from him while he was taking a shower. And whoever it was, knew a dirty rotten secret that would be the undoing of Dr. Benson. Who is Tommy B.?

Who was on the short list of people who could write that message? Dr. Benson had a good idea of who that was, but then again, how could he know about Tommy? Patrick. With the manner in which Jimmy was killed and now this? Dr. Benson had been lying to himself. He had been lying to himself this whole time; he was just too afraid to admit it. He had zero evidence, but he was certain it was Patrick.

THIRTEEN

"I was a mistake of nature, a mad beast."

-Andrei Chikatilo; 56 victims; Yabluchne, Ukrainian USR

Monday morning had come quickly, and Gladys looked like she had seen better days. Her lack of sleep over the weekend had taken its toll. Working on her quilting projects and drinking tea were the only way to keep her mind off Arthur.

"Ask her to come over, Arthur," Patrick whispered from the rec room.

"What for?" Arthur replied.

"Just do it. She looks a little rattled. I'd like to have a chat with her."

The rec room had the usual suspects. Old George was staring out of the window and into the courtyard, smoking a cigarette and cursing at himself or someone else who wasn't there. There really wasn't much to look at since the maintenance crew had recently turned off the water to the fountain because of the early freezes they get this far north. Now the patients would just walk around circling it, zoned out, waiting patiently for it to turn back on.

"Hey, Mrs. Johnston," Patrick called from the rec room.

"Hello, Arthur. How are you?" Gladys said calmly. Although she was nervous around him, Gladys kept her cool and put on her best poker face.

"I'm good. Tell me something, Ms. Johnston. Where are you from?"

"Well, my family is from Louisiana. New Orleans."

"That would have been my guess based on your accent. Tell me something else."

"Sure, Arthur, what is it?"

"What's your greatest fear?"

Gladys just paused and pulled her hands from her white coat pockets.

"Why, Ms. Johnston, it's just a question. We're all afraid of something. So, what's your fear?"

"I…I don't know. Spiders I guess."

"Oh well, that's an easy one. You know there are only two spiders in North America that are deadly? That's right, the Black Widow and the Brown Recluse. Funny story, one summer a few years back I was stacking wood up for the coming winter. I reached into the pile of wood to grab a piece and felt a little poke on my finger. Wouldn't you know it was a Black Widow? Hurt like hell. You know what I did? I pulled the wood out frantically until I found her and I crushed her in the palm of my hand." Patrick gritted his teeth as he made a grinding motion with his hands. "Teach that bitch to bite me again."

"Wow, that's quite a story, Arthur." Gladys was now visibly nervous from the tone and demeanor that Patrick was displaying. Only she didn't know it was Patrick, to her it was Arthur.

"I have to run now. I think Dr. Benson needs me," she said as she started to walk away.

Patrick grabbed her by the arm and Gladys immediately reached into her pocket for her syringe.

"Hey, don't worry. I hear Black Widow bites are rare. Besides, it didn't kill me," Patrick said, smiling.

Gladys pulled her hand back and got free from his grip, storming off, half angry, and half terrified.

★★★★★★★★★★

"Dr. Benson? Do you have a minute?" Gladys asked.

"Yes, come in Gladys. What's the matter?" Dr. Benson said, taking off his glasses.

Gladys took a seat on the couch, and Dr. Benson walked over. He could clearly tell that she was a little upset.

"Dr. Benson, I'm scared. I don't know why, but I'm just really scared."

"Of what, Gladys? I've never seen you like this."

"I know. It's Arthur. He just gives me the creeps. And just now, he grabbed my arm." Glady put her hands out, palms down to show Dr. Benson how badly her hands were trembling.

"What did he say?"

"He asked me what my biggest fear was. But that's not it, he sounded…"

"He sounded what, Gladys?"

"He sounded different. He was acting differently. It just scared the shit out of me."

Dr. Benson went from semi-trying to calm Gladys down, to suddenly being extremely interested. He took a seat next to Gladys and grabbed her hands. "Did he say anything else?"

"No, he just said something about how he got bit by a spider once. That was it."

"Now, Gladys, I need you to remember. This is important. What did he call you?"

"What?" Gladys asked confused.

"What. Did. He. Call you? Your name, Gladys?" Dr. Benson said concisely.

"He called me Mrs. Johnston. Why is that important?"

A look of fear ran over Dr. Benson, and Gladys could immediately tell that something was wrong. "Dr. Benson! Why is that important?!"

He stood up slowly with his hands on his chin and walked away from her. "Because Gladys. Arthur has another personality named Patrick. Patrick is the one that kills people. Arthur calls everyone by their first name. Patrick calls them Mr. or Mrs. I've been trying to talk with Patrick, but I haven't had any luck."

"So, what does this mean?"

"It means the meds aren't working. It means his appetite to kill is still there. It means Arthur is no longer in charge."

"Gladys. Get Martin and Doug to help you, but calmly get Arthur up here. I'll have a little talk with him. You think you can handle that?"

"I think so, Doctor."

Dr. Benson walked up to her, grabbed her by her shoulders, and looked her in the eyes.

"Gladys, just be calm. You can do this. You're the best we have here. Now get tough."

"I'll bring him right up, Dr. Benson."

"Good. Now go."

★★★★★★★★★★

Dr. Benson was getting into quite a bit of a mess. He believed, and he was certain, that Patrick was now in control of Arthur and that somehow, Patrick was communicating with someone on the outside. Somebody had to be feeding Patrick, or rather Arthur, information and someone had to have broken into his house and written on the mirror. But how? Could Arthur and Patrick really have an accomplice on the outside? He didn't know. Dr. Benson couldn't exactly run to Detective Reynolds and tell him someone wrote on his mirror and that he thinks it's related to Arthur. It would undermine his control of his facility. And then there was the secret of Tommy B. If anybody found out about that, he was done. There was his conundrum. He couldn't run to the authorities, and he didn't have a clue how Arthur and Company were operating. His little castle was under attack, and if he didn't do something quickly, he would lose control.

As the trio shackled Arthur to the chair, Dr. Benson knew that this was not the time to show Arthur anything. He would play it all close to the vest and try to get as much information out of him as possible.

"Thank you all. You can go now. I'll phone for you when we are done here."

Dr. Benson straightened his glasses that were beginning to slide off his nose and walked around from behind his desk, gently sitting on the front part directly in front of Arthur.

"Hello, Arthur."

"Hello, Harold. "

"How have you been feeling?" Dr. Benson asked.

"I've been feeling rather good as of late. I just love the crisp, fall air."

"Yes, it's lovely in the fall here. No doubt."

"I was surprised to see you last Friday."

Dr. Benson astutely raised his eyebrows with confusion. Was Arthur admitting that he was in his house?"

"You look confused, Harold. You dropped by my cell on Friday evening. Do you not remember?"

"Ah, yes. Forgive me, Arthur. It was a long and taxing weekend. But I do like to walk around on occasion and check on my patients. I really do care about them, you know?"

"I know you do, Harold. Your passion for this place is evident."

"Tell me, Arthur. Are you a cat person or a dog person?" Dr. Benson asked.

"That's an odd question."

"Well, really it's not. It's something we learn in the early studies of psychology. I'd thought you'd know that."

"I don't know everything, Harold. But if I had to answer I'd say I was a dog person."

"Interesting. I thought for sure I had you pegged as a cat person. I personally prefer cats to dogs myself. Cats are fiercely independent. They can be left alone for extended periods of time. They aren't dependent on the affection of others. You see, when they want it, they take it. When they don't, they simply ignore you. They say that if you prefer dogs that you prefer to be the boss and in control. That you like something to be submissive to you, like a bitch. You understand?"

"Sure. Dogs are obedient. Man's best friend, right?"

"That's what they say."

"I guess you could say I'm just as surprised at your choice. Control. Isn't that what this place is all about? Or isn't that what you're all about?" Arthur rebutted.

Dr. Benson smiled in knowing that Arthur was trying to goad him. He would never admit it out loud, but it was working.

"Yes, in fact, it is, Arthur. Which is why I am thinking we are going to take your treatment to another level. Typical medicine just doesn't seem to be working on you. I believe that you are acting like it is, but we both know better. Isn't that right?"

"I think it's working just fine, Harold. I'm calm, lucid, and I'm not a bother to you or your staff. So, what seems to be the problem?"

"That's just the thing, Arthur, you are right. You aren't the problem, Patrick is. And since he won't show his face, well, we will have to treat the symptom and not the cause. That's not exactly my style of medicine, but desperate times call for desperate measures, Arthur."

"What does that mean for me?"

"Oh, I think you know. Electroshock therapy, Arthur," Dr. Benson said with a grin. "And if that doesn't work, a full-frontal lobotomy will be at my disposal shall I choose to use it. I think after that you'll be an obedient bitch, don't you? I like that. Well, what do you know, maybe I'm a dog person after all?"

Silence hung in the air as Dr. Benson pulled his trump card out and placed it on the table. In a game of mental wits, the tides were turning fast. Would they last? Tides always had a way of going back to where they came from. Besides, they were only there in the first place because of a powerful force called the moon. And in the case of Arthur

Fritz, he was the moon. And if he wanted ebbs and flows, he would have ebbs and flows.

"Gladys? Yes, come pick up Mr. Fritz and put him in his cell for the remainder of the day. No, that won't be necessary. He can eat in the morning. Thank you, Gladys."

"Have a good evening, Arthur," Dr. Benson gloated.

"You too, Harold," Arthur said somewhat sad and displeased.

FOURTEEN

"When this monster entered my brain, I will never know, but it is here to stay. How does one cure himself? I can't stop it, the monster goes on, and hurts me as well as society. Maybe you can stop him. I can't."

- Dennis Rader "The BTK Strangler"; 10 victims; Wichita, Kansas USA

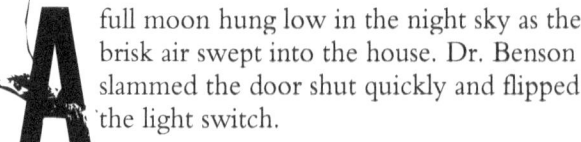

A full moon hung low in the night sky as the brisk air swept into the house. Dr. Benson slammed the door shut quickly and flipped the light switch.

"There you are, my good sir. Come here. It's been a long day," Dr. Benson said, sitting on his Danish lounge chair.

Cornelius jumped up on his lap and purred while Dr. Benson ran his fingers through his soft, orange coat. It seemed to glow almost a neon orange in the delicate, incandescent light.

"Yes, that's a good boy. How many mice did you catch today? I bet you got at least three, huh? Well, Daddy had a good day too. He batted around a mouse. He didn't kill it, he just toyed with it. I've seen you do it with them. You know what I'm talking about." Dr. Benson stretched his legs and

let a big, long sigh out while he stroked his beloved
Cornelius.

"We've had visitors, and we need to be
careful Mr. C.," Dr. Benson said while pulling out
something from inside his coat pocket. It was a snub
nose .38 revolver. He continued to stroke Cornelius
with his left hand and sat the revolver down on the
end table with his right hand.

"Bourbon, Mr. C. Good old-fashioned
bourbon," he said, pouring some into a small glass
from the decanter on the table.

Dr. Benson took a long drink, making his
face wince, and his lips tighten from the strong elixir.
"You never can be too careful, can you?" he said as
his eyes panned the room.

Making his way around the house, Dr.
Benson inspected all the windows to make sure they
were tightly locked, and double checked the doors.
Everything seemed to be all buttoned up. Dr.
Benson was used to being lulled into a false sense of
security. The bourbon didn't help his ego feel
stronger as he sat the gun on the toilet seat and took
the final swallow left in his glass. The small room was
already filling with steam as he stepped into the
flowing hot water, still humming the song he had in
his head from a few days back.

Dr. Benson reached down for some
shampoo and suddenly froze motionless where he
stood. He could have sworn he heard a noise. It
sounded as if the door was opening, but Dr. Benson
didn't want to believe that. He didn't want to think
someone was in his bathroom, and he certainly
didn't want to believe that it was Patrick. So, he did
the only thing he could do. Stand there and not

make a single sound. The water droplets were hitting the tub and ringing out into the room. The silence was finally broken by the sound of a creak in the floorboard; the telltale sign that someone was surely there. Did he risk going for the gun just inches away and confronting the person? Dr. Benson's illusion of control was completely gone as he shivered in the hot water, not knowing what was taking place in the very same room.

After what seemed like an eternity, Dr. Benson heard what was clearly footsteps walking out. Trembling in fear, he thought back and wondered what he did to deserve something like this. Maybe Tommy B. had something to do with it. Twisting around slowly, he shut the water off and carefully peeked around the back of the curtain to see if the revolver was still there. A small wave of relief ran over him to discover that it was. At least whoever was there wasn't there to kill him. Mustering all the courage he had, Dr. Benson clenched his muscles and yanked the shower curtain back to see what the message was this time, and it was loud and clear. They weren't playing around with him anymore. This time it wasn't a practical joke. This time they were playing for keeps.

"No!!!" Dr. Benson screamed out.

He screamed so loud that a vein was bulging from his forehead as the tears ran down his cheeks. Even some spittle hung from his top lip and onto his bottom as he sobbed. There in the sink was his beloved Cornelius, torn to shreds with a kitchen knife. Chunks of meat with pieces of his beautiful orange fur now tainted with deep, cherry red, blood stains. And on the mirror, written in blood read:

Who is Tommy B.?

A cold breeze ran through the house. Not because the furnace wasn't lit, but because Cornelius's killer left the front door open. The view from outside, through the front door, showed a scared and shaken little man, standing in bewilderment and wearing only a towel. With the gun in hand, Dr. Benson scurried to the bedroom and quickly put on some clothes. He ran to his coat in the living room and found the card that Detective Reynolds had left him.

"Detective Reynolds speaking."

"Detective. This is Harold Benson."

"Dr. Benson? It's late. Is everything okay?"

"Not really. Someone broke into my house and killed my cat. In my bathroom, while I was taking a shower."

"I'm sorry to hear about that, Dr. Benson, but why did you call me? You should have called the central office."

There was a long silence. In his haste to get someone out there, Dr. Benson forgot that he couldn't mention he suspected Patrick in all of this.

"No, you're right, Detective. I'm sorry. I was just shaken up and didn't think I guess."

"It's okay. Dr. Benson, does this have anything to do with Arthur?"

"No. Why would you ask that?"

"Just checking. You sound disturbed. And with good reason. But I'm just doing my job."

"Yeah…No, I…You're right. I'm sorry. I'll file a report first thing in the morning."

"Dr. Benson?"

"Yes?"

"Are you in any trouble? Cough once if you're in distress."

There was a small pause before Dr. Benson piped up.

"No, Detective. It's nothing like that. Thank you. Have a good night."

Dr. Benson hung up the phone and realized what a huge mistake he made. He could tell that Detective Reynolds suspected something was wrong.

"Fuck!" he stammered to himself in the empty and hollow room.

Fuck indeed…

The next day, you could hear a mouse sneaking around at New Hope Psychiatric Hospital. A cold front had come down from the Artic, and not much was moving around, not even the patients. The only one who wasn't in his cell was Old George. He was on his fourth Camel, and the third conversation with God knows who. Jimmy was dead. Gladys was shaken. And Dr. Benson had no idea what the hell was going on.

★★★★★★★★★★

June 9, 1967

It's been a while since the demise of Miles Worther. I feel I know why. I want a worthy opponent.

Something about these people has seemed easy. I go back to being the lion. Yes, they thin the heard. Yes, they go after the weak and sick ones, but I imagine every once in a while, they have to send a message to the rest of the safari. Something bigger than themselves. Something that can't happen quickly. I need a long game. But that doesn't mean I can't toy with a weak one every now and then.

—Patrick

June 18, 1967

Out hunting deer late last night and I saw something. I saw something wrong. Something I don't even want to write about. I only pray that Arthur didn't see it. I think I found my rival. And he is a worthy one at that.

—Patrick

June 27, 1967

Some days I enjoy wandering around town, taking in all the people as they go through their day. I wonder how many have thoughts like me? I stumbled upon a city council meeting at the New Hope City Hall. I sat quietly in the back as to not attract too much attention. They were announcing the new project that would start west of town—the New Hope Psychiatric Hospital. The mayor was up there talking about how New Hope was the perfect town for this type of hospital. New Hope was rural enough that the hospital would be secluded and it would bring about lots of jobs for our town. I guess I agreed with him. But that wasn't the exciting part of the meeting. This man came up to speak. A middle-aged doctor that went by the name of Dr. Harold Benson. It was when I heard him talk that I knew...he was driven. He came from upstate New York and wanted to make a difference in the world. I could see his passion for his profession, but I could also see his greed. He wanted to use New Hope to make his mark in the world. Besides all that, the thing that drew me to him was his intelligence. He was well spoken, and he was convincing. It was that very moment that a hunger inside me raged...like a fire that somebody dumped gasoline all over. But this Dr. Benson is different. He's not the kind of man you just take out. You must study him. This is the long game I spoke of. While the fire burns out of control, I will just have to bear the heat now.

—Patrick

August 19, 1967

The New Hope Psychiatric Hospital broke ground today. I found myself a job with a construction crew, working with the masonry unit. I will be laying brick for the first part of the development, and after that, they plan on putting me to work on the inside. This is going to work out beautifully. I

will practically have the keys to the castle. Not
practically. Literally.

—Patrick

****

"Gladys?"

"Yes, Dr. Benson?"

The phone line emitted a slight echo in it as
Gladys replied.

"Get Martin and bring Arthur up here, will
you?"

"But your session isn't until later this week."

"Dammit, Gladys. Just get him up here."

"Right away, Doctor."

FIFTEEN

"My consuming lust was to experience their bodies. I viewed them as objects, as strangers. It is hard for me to believe a human being could have done what I've done."

-Jeffrey Dahmer; 17 victims; West Allis, Wisconsin USA

"**H**arold! I'm really beginning to like these impromptu chats. I just never know what's going to come up."

"Shut the fuck up, Arthur!" Dr. Benson barked as soon as his staff left.

Arthur recoiled in surprise. "Harold! What is the problem?"

"Stop with the fuckin' 'Harold' shit! I want to know what Patrick is up to!? I know you know."

"But, Harold, I don't know. Honestly. The guy is what got me here in the first place. He has a mind of his own."

"Is he here now?!" Dr. Benson asked scanning the room. "Hey, you chicken shit! Show your face."

"He's not here, Harold. But I know one thing."

Dr. Benson paced around the front of his desk trying to maintain his composure. He hadn't been this upset in a while. Suddenly, when Arthur said those words, he stopped in his tracks.

"He will be seeing you real soon."

Arthur sat still and content with his hair neatly parted to the right and his shoes in perfect position in front of him.

"Has he told you anything about a Tommy?"

"No, he hasn't."

"Look, you're a smart guy. You know that Patrick is a figment of your imagination. So, the information he has, you should or could theoretically have. You get that right?"

"I do get that. But I'm sitting here telling you that I don't know anything. I already told you that I was apprehensive about him killing people, but he made it sound convincing. You've got to understand that I can't help you now."

"Don't fuck with me, Arthur. I know you two are planning something. Besides, I'm supposed to be helping you, you little shit!"

Arthur sat with a blank expression as if he had nothing useful to say.

"Hey! Look at me! What are you guys planning?"

"I can't answer that, Harold. I just can't."

"Yeah? Well, it seems that you don't know shit, do you? It seems you have no useful information up in that brain. I guess it's time for the basement. Do you know what happens in the basement, Arthur?"

"I'm sure I could guess."

Dr. Benson slid out from in front of Arthur, cheeks still red from yelling, and over to his filing cabinet. Arthur just watched as Dr. Benson pulled a file from one of the drawers. He sat down at his desk and grabbed a pen and read aloud as he wrote.

"Patient Arthur Fritz does not seem to be responding to medication as expected. He has been increasingly hostile toward the staff and the other patients. I am recommending he be treated with electroshock therapy as the latest results seem promising for similar patients." He slammed the file shut and looked Arthur in the eye.

"You happy now? Since you don't seem to recall anything, what does it matter if we run a few thousand volts through that empty head?"

"You're the doctor, Harold. This is your domain. I can't make that decision for you."

"Oh, but you did. Your silence is making it for you. All I want to know is what he's up to. Or, to talk to him."

Arthur had no more to say. He sat there silently waiting for Dr. Benson's rant to end.

"You know what? I'm done with you. Get the fuck out of my face. I'll see you in the basement in a few days." Dr. Benson was starting to lose

control and reacting in the only way he knew; anger
and desperation.

★★★★★★★★★★

The basement had a swampy persona to it,
adding the eeriness of the entire place. It wasn't so
bad during the day, but at night when all the
maintenance staff was gone, it was lonely. Sometimes
all you could hear were the screams and moans of the
electroshock patients echoing through the hallway
down the brick-laden walls. It was late in the
afternoon, and Dr. Benson had finally calmed down
a bit to think rationally. He was traveling to the
boiler room where all the engineering documents
were kept. His session with Arthur had him rabid
and on a mission. Neither Arthur nor Patrick were
going to continue with this. Dr. Benson certainly
wasn't known to be a fighter, but when someone
kills his beloved Cornelius, that is when the line is
crossed. He didn't actually want to hurt Arthur, but
he needed Patrick; he needed to talk to Patrick to
characterize a psychopath for his life's work.

Dr. Benson used his master key to open the
boiler room door. It was as muggy as expected
inside. To the left was a large boiler that was used to
heat the entire building. Toward the back were
assorted tools on the wall and in the left corner was
what he came to look at. The only light that lit the
place was a dim bulb hanging from the ceiling. It had
a slight sway to it as if the swampy air was pushing it
around. Dr. Benson walked up to the tall and wide
file cabinet that held all the building plans. He began
to open each one until he found the ones he was
looking for.

Spread out on the work table, Dr. Benson
ran his fingers and flipped through the old drawings

and papers until he came across a big sheet titled: Contracting Personnel. Since this was a government-funded facility, all records of who did what had to be documented. Dr. Benson stood up a little taller and slid the glasses back up his nose to focus.

Masonry Contract

Lead Contract: New Hope Mason Company
Lead Contractor: Paul Danfor
Others:
Brian Flannigan
Murphy Paulson
Alberto Sanchez
Michael Thomas
Patrick Leopold

Dr. Benson froze in his tracks when he saw the last name on the list.

"Fuck!" he muttered out loud.

He flipped through some more records until he came to the one he didn't want to see. The one that would confirm his darkest fear.

Cell and Lock Contract

Lead Contract: Vermont Lock and Key
Lead contractor: James Fenton
Installer: Patrick Leopold

Dr. Benson leaned over the table and wiped the documents into the air with his arm.

"Godammit! That mother fucker is getting out. I fuckin' knew it!"

Patrick was indeed getting out. Patrick was the one who knew about Tommy B. Patrick was the one who killed Cornelius. And there was nothing Dr. Benson could do about it. After a few minutes of wondering what to do, Dr. Benson picked up the papers and tossed them on top of the filing cabinet. After never having lost control in his life, he had nothing. No point of leverage. Dropping his head, he walked to the back of the boiler room and into a cleaning closet. Behind the sink were a pack of cigarettes and some matches. He pulled out a Marlboro, lit it, closed the door, and leaned up against it facing the boiler. It made sounds like a monster trying to breathe, breathing in raggedly and struggling to exhale. The only other sound was a drip of water hitting the floor from a leaky pipe overhead.

Dr. Benson took in a long drag and stared at the cigarette. Almost everyone around the facility smoked, but he was the only one who smoked only when under duress. And right now, he was under attack. As he neared the last puff to call it a night, a metallic ringing sound clanged on the concrete floor and echoed in the empty room.

"Who's there!?" Dr. Benson called out.

There was no reply.

Dr. Benson stomped out his smoke on the concrete floor. "Who is that?"

The only reply was the water splashing as before. Dr. Benson slowly made his way to the door, never turning his back from behind the boiler, the place where he was certain the noise came from.

Grabbing the doorknob, he turned it slowly and
swiftly ran out of the boiler room and into the
hallway, leaving only the echoes of his footsteps
behind him.

★★★★★★★★★★

Dr. Benson had just endured quite an
afternoon. He confirmed that he was being stalked
by a demented serial killer that was supposedly
locked behind bars and medicated at the hospital that
he, himself, ran. What did Patrick want with him?
He wouldn't have to wait very long to find out.

The house was lonely and quiet without
Cornelius. There weren't any plants or other animals
to fill it because Dr. Benson didn't have time for
anything else. As he walked through his living room,
his first reaction was to sit in the chair and call for
Cornelius. Old habits die hard. Reality set in and
once again his heart was broken.

Dr. Benson poured himself a larger drink
than normal from the crystal decanter and poured
half of the glass down his dry throat in one gulp. It
burned all the way down and tingled his stomach
when it got there. Drinking on an empty stomach
only made the problem worse. Dr. Benson never
took another drink from the glass after that. He only
stared into his dark kitchen with the light
illuminating the back of his chair and his head.

"Let's put this day behind us," Dr. Benson
said as if trying to use psychological techniques to
sooth himself.

Sometime later, loud snores rang out into
the bedroom while Dr. Benson was out cold. His
glasses lay on the nightstand next to his bed, and his

clothes were tossed randomly on the floor as if he had been out all night binge drinking. The curtain was drawn, but the moon still managed to break between the glass and the wall, revealing small details in the room. Just past the foot of the bed in the corner of the room sat a resting chair next to a dresser. In that chair sat a calm and smooth demeanor that was never out of control.

"Those things will kill you, you know?"

Dr. Benson shuffled in his bed, not sure if he had heard a voice or was just dreaming.

"Wha?" Dr. Benson said half-asleep.

"I said those things will kill you."

"What things?" Dr. Benson was thoroughly confused at this point, but starting to wake up.

"Cigarettes. They'll kill you."

Dr. Benson reached for the lamp on the nightstand and clicked it on. In the corner chair sat a shadowy figure with his legs crossed. Without his glasses, Dr. Benson couldn't quite make out who it was. Putting them on made it very clear.

"Arthur!?" Dr. Benson said, pushing up against the headboard and sitting up straight.

"I'm sorry, Dr. Benson. Arthur isn't here right now."

#

"After my head has been chopped off, will I still be able to hear, at least for a moment, the sound of my own blood gushing from my neck? That would be the best pleasure to end all pleasure."

-Peter Kurten; 9 victims; Mülheim am Rhein Germany

"**P**atrick?" Dr. Benson asked.

"The one; the only," Patrick replied from the shadows.

"Wha…What are you doing here?" Dr. Benson asked nervously.

"Isn't this what you wanted? Didn't you want to meet me?

Dr. Benson struggled for words as his hands trembled in his lap.

"I want to help you. To treat you. But not here Patrick. Not like this, in my bedroom."

"I'm sorry, Dr. Benson. You weren't clear. But we will have our little sessions like this from now on. And you are free to ask me anything you want."

There was a long silence as Patrick stared into Dr. Benson's eyes, never breaking contact, never blinking. Finally, in the act of defeat, Dr. Benson dropped his head.

"I...I.."

"What, Dr. Benson? Get it out, man!" Patrick said, raising his voice.

"Why are you doing this to me?"

"Oh, Dr. Benson. You're like a freshman. Going right for my pussy. You need to warm me up first. Get me excited. Kiss my neck. Don't be such an amateur."

"What are you talking about?" Dr. Benson asked.

"Why do you watch movies?"

"I don't know, for entertainment," he replied.

"You really need to calm down and focus. If I wanted you dead, you'd be dead right now. We watch movies because we want to feel the drama. It makes us feel alive. It's a parody of our own lives. Now tell me, Dr. Benson, do you feel the drama now? Are you alive?"

The old wooden chair squeaked in the silent room as Patrick shifted his weight to the opposite side. Dr. Benson was staring at what he only knew to be Arthur, but now he was talking to the deranged Patrick Leopold. Dr. Benson couldn't move from fear. The only thing going through his mind was, *where is my revolver?* It was in his jacket that happened to be draped over his nightstand, next to Patrick.

"I do feel alive, Patrick."

"Oh, Dr. Benson, you're stalling. The tone of your voice is telling me your brain is thinking of something else. Maybe it's wondering where that .38 snub nose pistol is. Maybe it's wondering if I have it. Well, I'll put your mind at ease. I have it."

Dr. Benson's head dropped in discouragement, knowing he was trapped.

"Are you going to kill me? Did my soul tell you that it wants to die?" Dr. Benson asked.

"I am not going to kill you, Dr. Benson. And no, your soul hasn't talked to me."

"Then what do you want with me?"

"I want to study you. I've been fascinated with you ever since listening to you at city hall one day. You're smart. You're the top guy in your field. And you're obsessed with guys like me. I guess it's fair to say I'm obsessed with men like you."

"So, if you're not going to kill me, then what's to stop me from going to the authorities? Or keep you in solitary confinement in the basement for the rest of your days?"

"My knowledge of Tommy B. is what's going to stop you from doing all that. I have everything anyone needs to know about that, all packaged up and ready to go to the press if that should ever happen. It's either that, or I'll shoot you in the face with your own gun in front of your staff."

"What do you know about Tommy?" Dr. Benson asked.

"Not what I know about him, what I know about you. And if you want to test that, then let me know. But until then, we will continue to have these sessions."

"Here?"

"Yes, here, Dr. Benson. Where else?"

"Well, my office of course. Where you can get the proper care?"

"That's a tired message, Dr. Benson. You think shocking poor Arthur is going to help give him, or me, the proper care? Sticking a needle in and scrambling my brain? No, that's not how we get you better."

"Get me better?" Dr. Benson asked puzzled.

"Yes, you're sick, Dr. Benson."

"Patrick, I'm sorry, but you are the one that is sick. You don't exist. You're Arthur. I know he's inside there somewhere."

Patrick's face took the form of a scowl from the doctor's comments. He stood up slowly and started to walk toward Dr. Benson. The floorboards creaked in the old house as the distance between the two men closed. Patrick pulled a small kitchen knife out of his front coat pocket. The light from the lamp reflected onto Patrick's face. His white teeth peeked out from his curled lips as he put the blade to Dr. Benson's neck.

"You feel that cold steel doctor? Is that real? I can see your carotid artery pulsing through your wrinkly skin. Do you always get so excited from things that don't exist?"

"I'm sorry, Patrick. That's not what I meant."

"We have so many things to correct, Dr. Benson. It's good we have time to get you better. And if we can't get you better, then you have no use for this world."

"I'm sorry, Patrick. Just please don't hurt me," Dr. Benson said, starting to cry.

Patrick moved the blade up to Dr. Benson's chin and flicked it against the skin quickly, making a small trail of blood run down his neck.

"You touch Arthur in the wrong way, and you're dead. You tell anyone about any of this, and you're dead. Understand?"

"Yes, Patrick. I promise."

"You know what I'm capable of. You've seen the pictures. Too bad the blood looks black in those photos. It's such a bright and glorious red in real life. You've read the reports, too. And just think, I was an amateur then. Imagine what I am now."

"Just don't hurt me. Please."

"Oh, there will be pain, Dr. Benson. Without it, there is no evolution. No growth. Pain is essential, a necessity for everything. It's coming. Embrace it. I'll see you at our next session, Dr. Benson. Sleep well."

Patrick stood back up from leaning over Dr. Benson and quickly slid out of the house. The door slamming echoed through the empty house as Dr.

Benson shook like a wet dog in the wind. He didn't
sleep another wink the entire night, and with good
reason. Patrick, the disturbed lunatic split personality
of Arthur Fritz, was now in control. He was in
control of everything. This was not the kind of
position that Dr. Benson was used to being in.

★★★★★★★★★★

"Good morning, Dr. Benson."

"Good morning, Gladys," Dr. Benson said
in a somber tone. "Hello, Martin."

"Hello, Dr. Benson," Martin replied.

Dr. Benson had passed the two in the
hallway.

"You okay, Dr. Benson?" Gladys asked.

"Yeah, I'm fine. I didn't sleep very well last
night."

"Looks like you cut yourself shaving too,"
Martin interjected.

Confused, Dr. Benson didn't recall cutting
himself, but he quickly realized what she was talking
about as he reached toward his chin to find a small,
red scab on his otherwise clean face.

"Oh, that. Yeah, clumsy I guess. Do you
mind getting me some coffee and sending Arthur up
please?" he said, walking toward his office.

"No problem. Hey, Dr. Benson?"

He swung around to see what Gladys
wanted. "Yes?"

"You are doing great work with him. You're gonna be the best you know that? World renowned," Gladys said, trying to shrug off some of that previous fear and show some confidence.

Dr. Benson could only smirk. They saw the tiredness in his face and eyes and wanted to continue to champion their boss, knowing he was striving for that spotlight, but they didn't know how far from that he was. They didn't know that the cut on his chin came from his own kitchen knife at the hand of a serial killer that was under his care. What a spot he was in.

"Thank you, Gladys. And be careful with Arthur," Dr. Benson said quickly and walked off to his office.

"So, how do you like it here so far?" Gladys asked Martin.

"It's good, you know? I mean Dr. Benson is great. I get paid well. I like the rest of the staff. It's good. Douglas has really been a great friend to me."

"Yeah, he's been around. I had worked with Douglas before this place was even built. Those were crazy days, let me tell you," Gladys said in her thick, southern drawl.

"But I like it here, you know. I feel like I'm starting to really fit in and be part of the family here. I'm finding myself. Although I can't imagine being that confident like you."

"You just stick with me and Douglas, and you'll be fine."

"Hey, do you mind if we get a quick smoke before bringing Arthur up?"

"Yeah, but make it fast. We don't want to keep Dr. Benson waiting too long."

They took a small detour on the way to Arthur's cell to a break room for the staff up on the second floor. Martin took out a cigarette and lit up in the small room. He extended the crumpled-up pack to Gladys, but she just shook her head in disgust.

"Those things will kill you, you know?" Gladys said.

"Yeah, well eventually something has to, right?" Martin said with a smile on his face.

"Who got you on those things anyways? Was it Douglas?"

Martin just shook his head while he leaned against a small sink, his black shirt coming untucked from under his white orderly coat.

"And tuck that damn shirt in, Martin."

"Damn, Gladys. You da' meanest but coolest boss I've ever had."

"I'll whoop your ass like a boss, Martin."

Martin smiled with the cigarette in his mouth while Gladys just stood there with her arms crossed.

"Come on, Gladys. You're tough as nails, but what gets you?"

"Nothin'. But you're the second person to ask me that."

"Who was the first?"

"Arthur."

"Oh shit. Arthur Fritz asked you that?"

"Yeah. Scared the shit out of me. But don't worry about that. Just stick to our procedures and be calm around him."

"I got it."

"C'mon, let's not keep Dr. Benson waiting."

★★★★★★★★★★

Gladys peeked through the glass before inserting the key into the cell door. Arthur was laying in the bed in the fetal position with all his clothes on.

"Good morning, Arthur. You alright? They said you didn't eat breakfast today."

Arthur slowly shifted around to look at them. Patrick was sitting on the desk, swinging his legs like a kid without a worry.

"Oh, hi Gladys. Hello, Martin," Arthur finally said.

"You okay?"

"Yes, I just didn't sleep last night."

"Dr. Benson wants to see you."

Arthur stretched and yawned while Patrick swung his legs impatiently.

"Tell them, Arthur," Patrick said, finally speaking out.

"Tell them we just saw him last night. Ha, ha, ha," Patrick said with an eerie laugh.

"Stop that, Patrick. Stop looking at him like that," Arthur said aloud.

"He dies tonight, Arthur."

Martin and Gladys stared silently at each other while Arthur spoke to the air.

"You ready to go?" Gladys asked.

"Yes."

Martin shackled Arthur to the chair while Gladys towered over both, right hand in her pocket stroking the only weapon they had against a crazed patient.

"There you go," Martin said calmly to Dr. Benson.

"Thank you, Martin. Gladys," Dr. Benson said, nodding his head.

"Good morning, Harold. You look as tired as I do."

"Yes, maybe that's because we were both up late last night."

Dr. Benson was in a calm mood despite having a knife at his neck only hours ago. He had stayed up all night wondering how he would get through this situation and get through it alive. The only answer he kept coming back to was Arthur. He would work free of this situation through Arthur.

"Yes, well I'm certainly sorry for that," Arthur said blankly.

"It's okay. This is why we are here, to help you."

"You can't say I didn't warn you, Harold. I told you how he was. I told you that you might regret what you wished for."

"I know, Arthur, and thank you. But you have to realize that you are sick. We need to get you better before Patrick destroys you."

"Destroys me? Everything he does is to protect me. How is he going to destroy me?"

Dr. Benson didn't have an immediate answer. He just stared at Arthur's empty, cold eyes. "Patrick wants to kill me, doesn't he?"

"I think you know the answer to that, Harold."

"He said he wouldn't."

"Patrick says a lot of things. Some you can trust, some you can't."

"Is he here?" Dr. Benson asked.

"He certainly is, Harold."

Dr. Benson's eyes wandered around the room and settled into the back corner where Patrick usually stood during their sessions.

"Patrick?" Dr. Benson called out. "Can we talk here? I feel we can make more progress."

"He's not going to talk here, Harold. It's not his style."

Dr. Benson's face began to turn a deep red. He had held his composure as long as he could, but the fear of constant threat was building like a bomb until his loss of control became too much.

"You won't show your face when you're tied up!? Come out, Patrick, you fuckin' coward!"

"Now, Harold, you know nothing good will come of that. Besides, he's not back there," Arthur said, turning his head from behind him and staring directly above Dr. Benson. "He's standing right over you again."

SEVENTEEN

"I saw the light over the confessional and the voice said, 'That's the person to kill.'

-Herbert Mullin; 13 victims; Salinas, California USA

It was just after two in the morning, and Dr. Benson had finally fallen asleep when the creak of a floorboard caught his attentive brain and woke him up. A chirping cricket could be heard outside the window as Dr. Benson rose quietly and reached for the light. He let out a long and disappointed sigh when he saw the shadowy figure in the corner again.

"Patrick?"

"Good evening, Dr. Benson," Patrick replied.

Dr. Benson reached for his glasses and was fully awakened by something more than just Patrick being there.

"P…. Patrick. What's that on your face?" Dr. Benson mumbled.

Patrick wiped his cheeks with his hand and looked down to see semi-dried blood on his fingers.

"Oh, that. That's blood, Dr. Benson."

"Whose blood Patrick!?"

"Martin's blood."

"Oh fuck. Patrick, did you kill him?"

Patrick just laughed, giving Dr. Benson the answer he already knew.

"Why are you killing these people Patrick? Why my staff?"

"Well, Dr. Benson, because I love it. I love killing people. Do I need any other reason besides that? And if I gave you one, would it warrant what I've done?"

"Fuck, you're going to kill me, aren't you?"

Patrick didn't answer, he just pulled a handkerchief from Dr. Benson's bureau and wiped his hands and face.

"This is our first formal session, Dr. Benson. Are you ready?"

"For what?" Dr. Benson replied.

"For the healing. Shall we start with your aggressive behavior today with Arthur?"

"What are you talking about?"

"You beat up on Arthur to get to me, Dr. Benson. You screamed out for me. Well, here I am."

"I'm...I'm just being harassed. How am I supposed to react? Just give up? I need out of this situation before it gets worse. Please, Patrick."

"You're right."

"About what?"

"About being held hostage and things getting worse," Patrick said smiling.

The sobs coming from Dr. Benson echoed in the dimly lit room. Patrick just laughed until Dr. Benson finally realized he was talking to a lunatic. The doc was motionless. Invoking his imagination, he pictured the bloody and macabre images he read about in the reports and pictures, and he put his face where the victim's face was. Patrick didn't kill people in a clean and quick way. He prolonged the merger between death and life.

"Well, I don't like this, but let's talk," Dr. Benson said.

"Good. So, let's talk about your constant need for control. That's a good place to start."

"Can I tell you something?"

"Sure, Dr. Benson."

"You're deeply disturbed, do you know that?"

Patrick paused to think about what Dr. Benson had just said. "Yes. I do know that, and I apologize. I imagine in another life I'd be a pirate. Not the kind that robs and steals. The kind that lays around and drinks all day. Anyway, let's talk about your need for control?"

"What?"

"Dr. Benson, you need to focus. You are of no use to me if you don't talk. And if you are no use to me, then why are you alive?"

"Okay. Okay. I mean, I don't know. Who doesn't like control? You seem to like it."

"Let's not turn this on me. This is about you. Always has been. Is your need for control the reason for Tommy B.?"

"I don't know what you're talking about, Patrick."

"Oh, Dr. Benson, stop. You're making a fool of yourself. Thomas Buselli. You know exactly who he is. He lives over on Viola Avenue just behind the elementary."

"What about him? That was a long time ago."

"Let's ask him if he feels like it was a long time ago. Fucking an eight-year-old boy, Dr. Benson? With the Mayor? And I'm the sick one? I could fill this room up with loving mothers, and I wouldn't be the only killer in here."

Dr. Benson lowered his head in shame. Patrick certainly knew his secret and could destroy his whole life.

"I mean it's pretty obvious. You live alone, and you have a cat…had a cat…Sorry."

Dr. Benson started crying again, tears running down his cheeks and into his flannel pajamas.

"Yes, Dr. Benson, we have a long way to go, don't we? A long hill to climb. I told you it was going to be painful. Let's hear it. Stop crying and tell me about little Tommy B."

"I don't know. You're right. I am sick. I need help," Dr. Benson sobbed. "I…like little boys. I feel like I can dominate them."

"Ah, there we go. Domination. You can grab him by his little wrist and hold him down easily, eh? How did you keep him from telling someone? Oh, I know. His father died when he was a baby, and you were there for him. Is that it?"

"I guess so. I just…it was Mayor Jenkins. I really cared about Tommy. Boys are just…my…our…weakness. But I'm a good person. I really want to help people like you."

"You think I need help? You've been planning to use me to rise for a long time now. You licked your chops when they found Arthur to be criminally insane. But guess what? I was licking my chops to get caught. What was your plan for me?"

"I was going to treat you. Write a book about the country's worst serial killer, and…"

"And what?"

"And be the most respected psychiatrist in the country."

"Let me tell you about a book. One day they will write a story about us, Dr. Benson. And it will be a glorious saga of the Great Doctor Benson and the Twisted Patrick Leopold. But before it gets written, tell me this: who amongst us will be the protagonist and who the antagonist?"

"I don't know," Dr. Benson mumbled.

"How are we going to fix this? Should we try pills? How about a lobotomy?" Patrick said, laughing manically. "How many people's brains have you scrambled?"

"I think five or six."

"You think!? The good doctor can't even remember? I know exactly how many people I killed. I at least cared about my victims enough to remember them. You simply just scramble them up and let them rot. That is torture. So, I ask again, Dr. Benson! Who amongst us is the protagonist and who the antagonist!? Who Dr. Benson! Who!"

"You are, Patrick. You're the protagonist."

Patrick smiled as if he was rewarded. "Our session is almost over, Dr. Benson. You've done well. I feel like we are making good progress. Let me leave you with this little secret, I, too, am a control freak. The thing about having control is to never lose it. You have lost it. But you didn't lose it tonight, or even last week. You lost it a long time ago. You lost it the day I bumped into you. The long game, Dr. Benson. Our meeting was no accident. This has been years in the works. See you next time. Sleep well, Dr. Benson."

Dr. Benson couldn't even answer. His head was spinning so fast. He had grossly underestimated Patrick's intentions. He felt like a deer being hunted by a master hunter. One who never missed. The kind that always brought home food. Did nature give Dr. Benson enough to survive man? He spent the whole night awake pondering that very question and the next, if any, move he had.

★★★★★★★★★★

Dr. Benson was at the hospital bright and early the next morning. He hadn't slept anyway, so he figured he might as well get some work done. He had been so distracted with all of the Arthur-and-Patrick business that his other patients around the hospital had gotten away from him. A federal inspection was coming in the next month, and he had plenty to do. The Federal Psychiatric Board would also be interested in the progress of Arthur Fritz.

"Gladys, how are we looking for next month's inspection?" Dr. Benson asked.

"We're in fantastic shape. I've taken care of all the staff records, and the facility is good. You have to update all the patient records, but other than that, I think we will be okay. No glaring problems."

"Good. Thank you, Gladys. I appreciate all of your hard work."

"Dr. Benson?"

"Yes, Gladys?"

"Are you okay? I mean, you seem distracted lately. Tired. I don't know. Maybe I'm overreacting, but I'm worried about you."

"Thank you, Gladys, but I'm fine really. I lost my cat recently, and I'm getting ready for this inspection. We are getting three new patients this month. It never stops. No need to worry. What about you? How are you coping with your bad feelings about Arthur?"

"Not good, Dr. Benson. Something about him creeps me out. I just feel something bad coming on. The way he talks to me."

"I know, Gladys. Just be careful around him. You'll be okay. Those are just feelings. The brain can lead you astray sometimes. It can make mountains out of molehills. I'm a doctor, trust me," Dr. Benson said smiling.

"I respect you as a doctor, I certainly do. But my grandma had these feeling, and she wasn't ever wrong. But you're right. I suppose I'll be okay."

"Why thank you, Gladys."

"Thank you, too, Dr. Benson. Hang in there. We gon' be alright."

★★★★★★★★★★

"Hello, this is Dr. Benson."

"Dr. Benson, Detective Reynolds here. How are you?"

"I'm great. Thank you."

Dr. Benson wasn't great. He knew what this call was about. He just didn't think it would be this fast. His mind wondered exactly what Patrick had done to him.

"Listen, we've identified a body that was found down by the river last night. He had a badge in his wallet for your facility. Are you missing anyone today?"

"Not that I know of."

"His name was Martin Dells. Black fella. You know him?"

Dr. Benson sighed out loud into the phone. "Yes, I know Martin. Damn it, Detective. What the hell is going on out there?"

"I don't know, but we've managed to keep the details of this one under wraps from the press. This is the second person that has turned up dead from your facility. I think we have a real problem here, Dr. Benson."

"I would agree with you. My staff is going to be in an outright panic."

"Your staff and this whole damned town. I'm under a lot of stress here. The Mayor is breathing down our necks."

"I know Mayor Don Jenkins personally. I'll give him a call."

"No, that won't work Dr. Benson. I need you to come down to the station so we can talk. We also need a positive ID on the body. Get down here today."

"Detective, I have a lot of things going on here."

"Dr. Benson, I'm asking. Next time I'll get a warrant to your facility. Something is going on over there, and I'm going to find out what one way or another."

"Okay. Okay. Relax. I'll be there in half an hour."

EIGHTEEN

"I took the right leg of that woman's body, from the knee to the hip took the fat off and ate it while he stared at the other girl. When I bit into it, she just urinated right there."

-Arthur Shawcross; 11 victims; Kittery, Maine USA

Dr. Benson couldn't remember the last time he was at the police station. With a northerly wind at his back, he tightened the scarf around his neck as he stepped out of his car and into the big, double doors of the New Hope Police Department building. The duty guard who was attending the front desk recognized Dr. Benson as a prominent member of the community.

"Dr. Benson. Hello," the policeman said.

"Hello. I'm looking for Detective Reynolds."

"How is that hospital of yours going?"

"It's well. Look, I'm kind of in a hurry here."

"I'm sorry, Dr. Benson. He's right around the corner there," he said, pointing behind him.

The painted cinder block walls made for a sterile environment that one would think of when they imagined a police station. Dr. Benson unraveled his scarf and carried it by his side, opening the door to a bullpen of little desks with a black phone and a stack of files on each one.

"Benson!" a voice called from the back. Detective Reynolds waved him down from a small office that had "Chief of Police" written on the opaque and blurry window. Dr. Benson nodded, acknowledging.

"We're back here. You want some coffee?"

"No, I'm fine. Thank you," Dr. Benson said, walking toward the back of the bullpen.

Inside the office was the chubby and jowly Chief of Police, surrounded by stacks of papers everywhere. The disarray nearly had Dr. Benson's OCD ready to act out by starting to clean the place up.

"Please, take a seat, Dr. Benson," Detective Reynolds said.

Dr. Benson took his seat next to Detective Reynolds, but not before shaking hands with the chief.

"Chief, you ever met Dr. Benson?"

"I think I have, but it's been a while. How do you do doctor?"

"I'm doing well, Chief. I believe you are right, we did meet a while back at a city function."

"Maybe you're right."

Chief Nelson had a deep and raspy voice, partially due to all the fat that lined his neck and face. It was as if his body had to struggle through his loose jowls to talk.

"Detective Reynolds and I were just discussing some things. We think we have a real big problem here, Dr. Benson. After the Arthur fiasco, it feels like it's starting all over again. We just calmed down the public by catching that monster. Now it seems he's back. So, we wanted to talk to you about it. Why do you think whoever is doing this is targeting your staff members, Dr. Benson?"

"I don't know, Chief. I really don't. Can you give me any of the details on Martin?"

"You sure you want to hear them? I'm barely getting over all the victims from the Arthur Fritz case and here they are again. And that poor Jimmy kid…my god. We think whoever did it bled Martin out right in front of him, watched him die. That is very sick and very personal, as you probably know, Dr. Benson."

"Yes, I know. I've read killing someone with a knife is the most personal way of killing someone, but they took it to a new level," Detective Reynolds chimed in.

"Any thoughts?" the Chief asked.

"On what?" Dr. Benson replied.

"On all of this shit. I worked the Fritz case, and this feels like the Fritz case. The crime scenes just have the feeling that evil was there. It's palpable."

"Well, I can tell you Arthur is confined and in my care. He's mellowed out on some medication, and we are progressing with his treatment. If you're thinking this has anything to do with him, I think you're wrong."

Lies. Dr. Benson had Tommy B. hanging over his head, and now he had to protect and lie for a sick individual, without remorse, named Patrick.

"Well, then Arthur has inspired a new generation of killers. Our whole world is going to shit! Call the cavalry!" the chief said sarcastically.

"What can I do to help Chief?" Dr. Benson asked.

"Well for starters, maybe you can help Reynolds here profile this new killer."

"Sure. I need to see the files on Jimmy and Martin."

The chief nodded to Detective Reynolds. "The last thing I want is the Feds up here, Dr. Benson. New Hope has always been a pleasant and friendly town. I've dedicated my whole career to making that so."

The chief gritted his teeth down and one last time, gave Dr. Benson a scowling look.

"I'm gonna ask you one more time Doctor because I respect you. Does this have anything to do with Arthur Fritz? I would just as soon put a bullet in his head or give him the chair, but that lousy doctor and judge found him mentally ill."

"He is mentally ill, Chief."

"Even better reason to kill the son of a bitch then!"

Detective Reynolds just smiled and nodded his head in agreement.

"I can assure you, Chief. Arthur Fritz has nothing to do with this. He is in my care."

"All right. Reynolds, get him copies of the reports and pictures."

Dr. Benson wouldn't need any of those things. He had just lied through his teeth, knowing full well that Patrick was out again and on the loose. Dr. Benson was certainly in a tight position. He couldn't help but think back to Patrick asking him who was the protagonist and antagonist. The deeper this whole thing got, the more he believed that maybe he was the villain. After all, Tommy B. wasn't his only victim. Nor was he alone…

"Here you go, Dr. Benson. I don't have to remind you to keep this confidential."

"I'll work on a profile write up for you as soon as I can."

"Thank you."

Detective Reynolds closed the door behind them as he and Dr. Benson made their way back into the bullpen area.

"Chief is a pretty tough guy, huh?"

"Yeah, he doesn't look like it, being a fat ass and all, but he knows his shit, and he'll protect this town no matter what. Now you see what I have to contend with."

"I'll be glad to help you."

"Thanks for your cooperation. We need to get this figured out soon."

"We certainly do," Dr. Benson said, referring to something else entirely.

"Let's get on over to the morgue and identify your guy," Detective Reynolds said.

★★★★★★★★★★

Dr. Benson and Detective Reynolds took the short ride through the town square, down a few blocks east and then across the river to the small hospital. They happened to cross the very river where Martin's body was found.

"Poor fella. He came from down south like a lot of other negroes, looking for work. He didn't have any family here really. Just Gladys and Douglas," Dr. Benson said of Martin.

"Who found him?" Dr. Benson asked as they walked to the morgue entrance behind the hospital.

"Some fisherman. Retired guy was up early this morning. He was kind of shaken up. We had to calm him down and make sure this didn't get out. But I think it's already stirring. The Mayor and the Chief are planning some sort of town meeting to try and stop this from blowing up."

Dr. Benson just shook his head in disbelief, mostly playing the part, but sincerely feeling sorry for Martin.

"I know you're used to this stuff, being a schooled doctor and all, but I'm just a small-time cop

in a quiet town, so I'm not. So just be ready,"
Detective Reynolds said.

They pushed through the stainless-steel
double doors and into the cold air of the morgue.
Dr. Greggs was there washing his hands in the big
sink to the left of the entrance. Dr. Greggs had a
stalky frame and stood wide as he scrubbed his thick
fingers in the soap and water.

"Hello, Greggs."

"Hello, Detective. You must be Dr.
Benson?" Dr. Greggs said with a smile.

"Yes, it's a pleasure to meet you."

"Same here. I've heard a lot about you. This
town is excited for you to put it on the map with all
that good work we keep hearing you're doing at the
hospital. Pardon the wet hands," he said, extending
his hand out.

"No problem about the hands and yes, thank
you. It's slow, but important what we are doing up
there."

Dr. Greggs walked over to one of the
coolers and opened the door. Inside was a body
covered with a white sheet. Dr. Greggs slid the tray
out, and Dr. Benson and Detective Reynolds
huddled around it.

"Did you perform an autopsy yet?" Dr.
Benson asked.

"No, we will get to that today. We needed
someone to ID and confirm the body first. And that
would be what you're here for."

"Yeah, he is. Let's get on with it," Detective Reynolds said sharply.

Dr. Greggs pulled the sheet back slowly to reveal the face and upper torso. He paused halfway and then continued to pull the sheet back all the way to his feet. Martin's dark brown body lay unperturbed and cold. He had a cut from one ear to the other. The cut was so deep that the head barely seemed to be attached anymore. Dr. Benson's eyes moved further down the body and saw he was also cut from his genitals all the way up to his neck. Dr. Benson grimaced and recoiled in disgust.

"Any clue which cut came first?" Dr. Benson asked.

"Definitely the long cut up the torso. The neck slashing is what killed him. So, whoever did this wanted him to feel some significant pain before he died. Disemboweling doesn't kill immediately. It certainly must have hurt like hell. Poor guy."

"You positively ID this guy as Martin Dells?" Detective Reynolds asked.

"Yeah, that's him," Dr. Benson said softly.

"All right. Let's get out of here. Thank you, Dr. Greggs."

"Anytime, Reynolds. Nice meeting you, Dr. Benson."

"You as well."

★★★★★★★★★★

After being dropped off at his car, Dr. Benson waited for Detective Reynolds to exit from view before making a B-line toward city hall just a block away. Dr. Benson needed to call in some reinforcements.

"Harold!" Mayor Jenkins said surprised.

"Don." Dr. Benson nodded.

"What is it? I have a lot on my plate today. Can it wait?"

"No. It can't wait."

Jenkins knew that look and immediately told his secretary to give him a few moments of peace. They went into his oak-laden office that even had a picture of him with President Eisenhower. Mayor Jenkins had been in politics for most of his life and was well connected. He came from D.C. and wanted to settle in a quaint town but still be actively involved in politics.

Jenkins was a dapper man, always seen wearing a three-piece suit and hair slicked with some form of hair treatment and neatly parted. His tall and slender figure helped physically demonstrate his ability to lead as he towered over most people with his six-four stature. Jenkins took his seat and lit up a cigarette, offering one to Dr. Benson. Reluctantly, Dr. Benson accepted.

"What is it, Harold? What's so important? I have a town hall meeting I'm trying to arrange before the people come up here and burn the damn building down."

"We go back a while. Right, Don?"

"More than I'd like to admit, Harold," Jenkins said laughing.

"Well, we have a little bit of a problem," Dr. Benson said, exhaling a large cloud of thick, gray smoke.

Jenkins perked up in his seat to give him more attention. "What Harold?!"

"Someone knows about Tommy."

"What?! Did Tommy say something to somebody? That little fucker. I'll kill him."

"No, he didn't say anything. Someone's been watching. They know everything."

"Who?"

"I can't tell you that, Don."

"Godammit, Harold. Do I have to remind you the positions we are in? I got your fuckin hospital built for you. You need to fix this situation, and fix it fast!"

Jenkins's face was bright red, and his perfectly aligned hair had somehow jolted loose from his outburst.

"Does he know about me, or is it just you?" Jenkins asked.

"I think just me. But with this guy, who knows?"

"Son of a bitch, Harold!"

"I'm handling it, Don. I needed to tell you about it. I needed some help."

"Well, if you can't tell me who it is, then how can I help you?"

"You're right. I panicked a bit. But I'll get it taken care of."

"You'd goddamn better, Harold. Everything we have ever done is at stake here. I won't let some snot nosed kid bring me down. Fix this mess, or I'll fix it for you."

"I said I got it, Don!" Dr. Benson yelled back. "Just watch your back. This person who knows is a little off."

"Do I need to worry? Do I need to get involved?" Jenkins asked.

Dr. Benson crushed out his half-smoked cigarette in disgust and shook his head. "No, not yet. I think I can get it under control."

"And if you can't?" Jenkins asked with a concerned look.

"Well, if I can't, we're fucked no matter what."

"Don't you fuck us, Harold. I'll bury you, you hear me?"

Dr. Benson didn't answer. He just maintained eye contact. He wasn't afraid of Mayor Jenkins. If Jenkins knew what the hell they were up against, he would pack up his bags and get the hell out of this town. Dr. Benson decided to spare the mayor the knowledge of Patrick until he could just make it go away himself. He had work to do. He needed a plan. How was he going to stop Patrick? It was as if he was always one step ahead of him. And he was.

★★★★★★★★★★

Gladys was waiting for Dr. Benson in the lobby of the hospital when he walked through the doors. She was sobbing and crying so much; her mascara was running down her face in black lines. Even Charlie, the security guard, was down and not his usual self. Word had quickly gotten around about Martin.

"Oh, Dr. Benson!" Gladys cried with her arms out.

Dr. Benson reluctantly took her into his embrace. "I'm sorry, Gladys. I know you cared about that young man," Dr. Benson consoled.

"What is going on here, Dr. Benson? I'm so scared."

"Gladys, let's go to my office and talk about this. Here isn't the place."

The last thing Dr. Benson needed was chaos amongst his staff. He had to get Patrick under control and shift his focus to himself and not to his staff. As Gladys took her seat, Dr. Benson tightened his lab coat around his waist. It was feeling loose and tightening it gave him something to be in charge of.

"Have a seat, Gladys. Try to relax. You are my star employee. You make things run around here."

"I know, Dr. Benson, but I'm losing it. That feeling, I told you. Something isn't right around here. Martin didn't deserve to die that young. Neither did Jimmy. They were young men in their primes," Gladys said, crying and sniffling.

"I know they were. I just got back from talking with the Chief of Police. He assured me they are working this matter with everything they've got. He also said we need to remain calm and vigilant."

"Is it him, Dr. Benson?" Gladys asked not wanting to hear a particular answer.

"No. You know that, Gladys. He's here. He's locked up.

"I know, but I'm hearing stuff, Dr. Benson. I'm hearing a copycat killer is trying to target people that work here to help get Arthur out.'

"Gladys, you know better than to listen to that garbage. He's in a locked cell with a three-inch, reinforced door. He isn't going anywhere. We just need to tighten up on procedures and security. Particularly for the inspection coming up. I need you healthy, Gladys. You're the rock around here. Get that mean, take-no-shit attitude back. Now get it together, Gladys!"

"I'm sorry Dr. Benson. I'll get it right."

"Now leave me be. I have some profiling work to do on this new killer," Dr. Benson muttered.

NINETEEN

"I do not really understand myself these days. I am supposed to be an average reasonable and intelligent young man. However, lately (I cannot recall when it started) I have been a victim of many unusual and irrational thoughts."

-Charles Whitman; 14 victims; Lake Worth, Florida USA

r. Benson locked the door behind Gladys, grabbed the envelope from atop his desk and headed over to the back of his room to sit on the couch. He got comfortable, adjusted his glasses and began to read the reports on Jimmy and Martin.

"Let's see how far off they are," he muttered to himself.

August 24, 1967

Work has been gratifying so far. I'm getting stronger from moving all this brick around. The paychecks are decent, but I should remind myself of the real reason I'm here. Dr. Benson. I saw him yesterday wandering around the construction site. He was wearing a white hard hat, which

symbolized management or authority. Everyone
else on the site wears a yellow hard hat. I can smell
the smugness on him. Walking around the place
like he owns it. Pointing at things that will get
done his way. Managing the managers. While I
hate him right now, I think when I get to know
him a little better I might just like the guy. But
with most people I like, they end up dead. I hate
him, but do I want to kill him? I don't know that I
do for certain. But if I did want to, the only
question is how? How do you end a man like Dr.
Benson? Slowly maybe. Maybe quick and sharp.
Although quick and sharp has not been my style
as of late. But I'm getting ahead of myself. It's the
fire raging inside that is making me even think
of all this killing business. I need to get to know
him better. Maybe I'll try to chat with him.

—Patrick

August 26, 1967

Well, I got my chance to talk to him today. I was
absolutely right. I hate him. He was walking
around as usual with the foreman. I acted like I
wasn't paying attention and I bumped into him
gently with my shoulder while walking by. He
did not take this lightly, oh no! The great and
powerful Dr. Benson couldn't be bothered. He hissed
at me while looking directly into my eyes. As if I
was some peasant in the way of his Lordship. I
asked him if he was the great Dr. Benson I had
heard of, but the foreman quickly interrupted that

conversation. I'm not sure Dr. Benson would have even entertained the question, but I was told to go back to work. That little bump was the closest I've been to him yet, and it made my loins tingle. It made my mouth water in anticipation of the blood that would be spilled. But I have to play this game right. And I believe that I am. The previous bodies are ready to be placed in spots that will lead back to me. I just need to get this hospital finished, so I have a warm place to call home while I get to know the great Dr. Benson even more. But he's a smart man. Not like the lifeless and dull saps I previously whet my appetite with. No, Dr. Benson would as soon lobotomize me and toss me in the dungeon before he lets me get to him. Every man has a weakness. Everybody has a vice. Mine happens to be killing people. To me no worse than laying down with a hooker. All a part of nature. It's there. We all have one...and I'll find his soon enough...

—Patrick

August 30, 1967

I've decided to start collecting some evidence on Dr. Benson. What I saw in June...well...I'd still rather not talk about it. I went down to the hobby store this afternoon and purchased a top of the line camera. It has a big zoom on it, so I supposedly can take pictures from far away. I spent some pretty good money on this, but it's what needs to be done. I can't keep going after the weak...well, I

can, but I need this. This is my trophy kill. This
the one I stalk for months or years if needed. The
one I study carefully on the outside before taking
apart his insides. The only issue is that I need to
get them developed somewhere. But if I get the
pictures I think I'll get, then I only need to get
them developed once. Which means I just have to
kill whoever works in the film lab that day! Just
when I was starting to lose the itch to kill someone.
I thought this long con with Dr. Benson would
wear on me and slowly grind me down to where I
didn't want to anymore. But no, my thirst has
returned with a vengeance. Tonight, I will play
with the camera, and this weekend I'll do some test
shots.

—Patrick

September 4, 1967

It was cool and breezy out today. After working
long, hard hours during the week, it's good to relax
and take my time on my real passion. I've been
reading the manual for the camera. It's quite
complicated, and there are many features that I
probably won't ever use or need. I packed a small
lunch today and took a hike through the woods.
Seeing all those trees makes me miss the days of
chopping wood. I have so much wood piled up I feel
like I would be okay trying to get through a
nuclear winter. With all this crazy talk of the
bombs, I just might need it. I made my way down
a trail and around Mrs. Denison's old property

line. It opened into a small clearing with a
trickling creek that ran down the middle. I've been
out here before, and I usually see lots of wildlife.
Today was no exception. In the meadow, I saw the
doe I spoke with a while back. I'm certain it was
her. She never saw me this time. I was able to
sneak through the tall grass and set up my
camera on her. I zoomed in and snapped away
some amazing shots. Or at least what I think will
be amazing shots. As I snuck through the grass
and got closer and closer to her, I felt the power of
the lion again. I felt a surge of energy in thinking
this is how I'm going to stalk Dr. Benson. The deer
had no idea I was even there. If I had been a real
lion, she wouldn't have known what hit her. Just
like Dr. Benson. He bumped into me last week...he
had no idea I was even there. Yes, he knew he
physically bumped into a person, but he didn't
know it was me. But he will...

—Patrick

September 5, 1967

I couldn't wait any longer to get my pictures
developed. I met the young lady at the photography
store where they process film. Come to find out
after chatting with her, she had just dropped out
college and had come back home from the west
coast. She was a rebellious one, trying to piss her
parents off mostly, who had done her share of
drugs and slept with more than her fair share of
men. It was a minor tragedy that she had to be

there that day, but the world wouldn't miss her.
She told me her name was Angie. Angie told me
that the owners of the shop lived upstate somewhere
and that they trusted her to run the place. She sure
was proud of her job. As I got to know her better,
my curiosity of the booming film industry
pushed her into showing me how it all worked. She
took me back to the developing room. It was
surprisingly dark in there. I suspected she wanted
to fuck me, but I didn't give her any indications
that I would. Besides, I knew I was going to kill her
before I even met her. The only question was how.
And after talking to her, I feel a pleasant and up-
close strangulation is in order. I spent the whole
afternoon laughing and talking to Angie. The
pictures of the deer came out wonderfully. I'd like
to take credit, but the folks at Kodak made it so
easy that anyone could do it. Now that I can take
pictures, it's time to stalk my prey.

—Patrick

September 8, 1967

The boss let us go at a decent hour today. We've
been working hard and are slightly ahead of
schedule. This is what I needed to get a jump on
my assignment. Dr. Benson left the construction
site around his regular time. I already had my
bag packed in my truck and had eaten dinner. It
wasn't much, just an apple and a thermos of
coffee. A cup of coffee could take me well into the
night as I'm more of a night owl anyway. I can

live on little sleep. I followed Dr. Benson from a
safe distance. I usually get excited about following
people, but this guy gets my heart racing. I want
to get to know him, the real him. I actually want to
hear his soul talk this time, his real, inner soul.
And I will...

As expected, Dr. Benson lives in an aristocratic
neighborhood. Neatly trimmed trees and delicate
lawns abound. The best part was that the back of
his house led out into the woods. Apparently, Dr.
Benson was sitting on a big parcel of land. After
careful thought, I decided to drive around back
through the federal land that borders his and keep
an eye from that angle. By the time I got into
position, the sun was setting. I couldn't have timed
it any better. I found myself a spot under a big
maple tree, and I drank some coffee. It was so hot
that steam was still rising out of the thermos. I sat
there for a bit wondering why I was so happy. I was
so happy because I was doing what I love. For
someone who didn't like killing people, this would
be a lot of work. But when you enjoy it, it's quite
fun. And I can say I'm having the time of my life.

Dr. Benson's house had a huge bay window
looking out into the trees. The blinds were drawn
tightly, but there was movement going on inside.
The lights started popping on one by one in
different areas of the house. I knew he was active
and moving around. I snuck the 500 yards from
the tree line to his backyard, just like I did with the
deer. It was beautiful. I had perfect cover from the
dark night and the large spaces between houses in

that area. I made my way over to one of the windows. It had a small gap between the sill and where the shades ended. Dr. Benson was in his living room, sitting in a very expensive and comfortable looking chair. On his lap was an orange cat. I could tell by the way he was stroking it that he loved it very much. In his other hand, he held a drink in a fancy glass. I could only assume it was liquor. He was drinking it neat. I like that. Why mess up a good drink with ice or anything else? I respect him for that. Just like those that drink their coffee black. Purists, maybe in a small form, but purists nonetheless. I watched into the wee hours of the night, but he didn't give me anything. If I have any redeeming quality, it's that I'm persistent. Persistent or worthless. The lion that loses its persistence dies. I will not die today.

—Patrick

September 9, 1967

The moon was out in full force tonight. I had to be even slyer this time around. I got to the woods behind the good doctor's house around ten. Some of the neighbors were still stirring about. The ones to his West were having some sort of late night cookout. I had a quick impulse to kill them all because they were disturbing my important work. But I had bigger fish to fry. Good thing Dr. Benson is a night owl like me. I assume he gets his best work done after everyone else is sleeping. Most

brilliant people are up late nights from my
observations on human nature. What was
discovered will not be taken lightly. Everyone has
their vice, including me. I live by this rule. After
the family next door settled in for the night, I
made my stalk toward Dr. Benson's house. He
made the mistake of not closing the blinds all the
way. With what he was doing, I would have been in
an underground vault. But I kill people for the fun
of it, so what do I know? I carefully peeked into the
window to see Dr. Benson nervously shuffling
around the living room. He was tidying up as if a
guest was coming over. But who has guests over
this late? Dr. Benson was wearing a dapper, three-
piece suit. He cleaned up well, to be honest. He
moved a vase of flowers over to his coffee table and
then downed a big gulp of liquor--Dr. Benson has
a penchant for the spirits too. This might work to
my advantage later. After he moved around the
house for what seemed like an eternity, the doorbell
rang. Dr. Benson tightened up his tie and parted
his hair with hands one last time before heading
over to the door. Who is the lucky lady you ask?
Oh, there was no lucky lady tonight. It was a
man...A man I've seen before. It was Mayor Don
Jenkins and another guest. What kind of guest?
The same one I saw back in June. The young kid
couldn't be more than ten years old. If I had to
guess, I'd say eight. Dr. Benson leaned down to
shake the boy's hand. The boy looked nervous, but
then again, so did Dr. Benson and Mayor Jenkins.
Dr. Benson ran to the kitchen quickly and came
back with a soda pop and offered it to the kid. The
kid refused it. Mayor Jenkins whispered

something into Dr. Benson's ear, and they all started off toward a room to the east end of the house. I scurried past some bushes and over to the other window where I found another sliver of a view through the curtain.

Dr. Benson sat the kid down on the bed and began to loosen his tie. Mayor Jenkins walked around the other side of the bed by the window and began to undress ...For a moment I felt sick to my stomach. I was merely a few feet away from these animals. In all the amazement of what I was about to see, I forgot my primary job. I quickly took the lens cap off and began snapping pictures of the action. I won't talk about what happened as I don't want to upset Arthur, but let us just say that Mayor Jenkins and Dr. Benson fancied little boys like the Romans did. After getting enough pictures, my job was complete. Time to get them processed.

—Patrick

#

"The only thing they can get me for is running a funeral parlor without a license."

-John Wayne Gacy; 33 victims; Chicago, Illinois USA

D r. Benson steamed down the hall and into the rec room, scanning the room for Arthur. An orderly happened to be in the area and met Dr. Benson near the center of the room.

"Hello, Dr. Benson," the young man said.

"Have you seen Arthur?" Dr. Benson asked.

"Yes, he's in his cell. Gladys ordered he be kept in there up until after the inspection."

"Thank you."

Dr. Benson headed straight for the stairwell and bumped into Old George.

"Watch it, you patsy! I'll kick your ass!" George grumbled.

Dr. Benson couldn't be bothered as he flew up the stairwell and into the long hallway of cells. Peeking in the window, he could see Arthur walking in small circles around the room, talking to someone, presumably Patrick. Dr. Benson grabbed his master key and unlocked the door, letting himself in.

"Well hello, Harold! I'm afraid you just cost me five dollars."

"How do you figure, Arthur?"

"Patrick said that you would be coming in here soon. I told him you were upset with us and there was no way you wanted to see us. I guess I was wrong."

"Yeah, well you just tell Patrick to be at the house tonight. We need to talk."

Arthur looked to the corner of the room where Patrick stood stoically sucking on his lollipop. Patrick gave Arthur a nod of approval.

"He'll be there, Harold."

Dr. Benson didn't reply, he just slammed the door behind him and marched back down to his office. Now he had to create a fake profile of a killer that didn't have the same *modus operandi* as Arthur. He had to hide the fact that it was Arthur until he could deal with the situation appropriately. Tonight would be a chess match with Patrick. He had to get some of the ground he lost back, but he didn't know how. All of Patrick's moves were premeditated, while Dr. Benson would just have to improvise and find a way.

★★★★★★★★★★

Dr. Benson couldn't sleep as he waited for Patrick to show up. The room was pitch black, but he listened intently for the telltale squeaking of the floor. Without having to wait too long, the wood floors started popping, and a shadow stood in the doorway. Before Patrick could take his seat in the corner, Dr. Benson flipped the light switch and was waiting there in the dark with his glasses already on.

"Hello, Dr. Benson. You're starting to like our little sessions, I see."

"Not exactly, Patrick. You are blackmailing me, for lack of a better word. I could almost say holding me hostage. How can I start liking this?"

Patrick gracefully walked over to his chair in the corner, never taking his eyes off Dr. Benson.

"I think in time you'll learn to love me. We have so much in common, except that I don't fancy little boys of course."

Dr. Benson sent over an annoyed look, mostly because Patrick was right and there was nothing he could do about it.

"So, what are we here for, Dr. Benson? This is your session. What do you want to do?"

"I want to talk about your killings."

"Okay. Anything is on the table here," Patrick said.

"How did you first discover you wanted to start killing?"

"Well it started off noble and with pure intentions, I guess you could say."

"Can you elaborate more on that?" Dr. Benson asked.

Patrick leaned in toward Dr. Benson with a smile.

"You see, Dr. Benson. This is what I was hoping for all along. You and I just sitting and talking, picking each other's brains, learning what makes me tick and what makes you tick."

Dr. Benson wasn't sure how to respond. Patrick made it sound as if they were two good ole' boys, shootin' the shit. That was his charm. He made it feel that way when in all actuality, he was virtually being held against his will. Dr. Benson thought that maybe this was why Arthur felt the way he did about Patrick.

"We just had a moment, Dr. Benson. Now, back to the killings. I think subconsciously when we realize we are doing something that others would think is wrong, we try to justify it. I tried to find a reason for it. But I couldn't. And when I didn't have an excuse for my actions, then came an awakening."

"Of what kind?" Dr. Benson asked curiously.

"A realization. A realization that there is an animal inside of all of us," Patrick said, giving off a smile of half evil and half sickness as he stared directly into Dr. Benson's eyes. "Now, tell me, Dr. Benson. Are you predator or prey?"

"I don't know the answer to that, Patrick."

"Oh, but I think you do. Little Tommy B. would consider you to be a predator. Would you agree?

"Maybe. And I guess you consider me to be prey?"

"That's a reasonable guess."

"So, you're going to kill me?"

"I haven't decided yet, Dr. Benson."

"What does it depend on?"

"On you telling the truth in our sessions. On you letting your true feelings out. On me getting to know you well."

"But you've never let anyone live. All of your victims died."

"Well…yes…but I change. Can I ask you a question? Do I scare you, Dr. Benson?"

"To my core, Patrick, to my core."

Upon hearing the response, Patrick squirmed in his chair with glee. A killer like Patrick lived for those words. They got him hard. They made his pulse quicken. He got off on that.

"As it should be, Dr. Benson. I'm a dangerous man."

"And suppose I just give you up to the authorities and take my chances with the Tommy situation?"

"If you're scared now, then I'd hate to see you when you did that. But make your move, Dr. Benson. I have six shots in your revolver. I'll wipe you and everything you know out before I go down. Besides, I've already been declared legally insane. I guess they might scramble my brain, but what good does that do you if I kill you?"

"None I suppose."

"Good. Then continue to play along until I tire of you and need something else."

"Very well. Can I ask you to do something?"

"What is that?"

"Tell me about Mr. Dale, Arthur's childhood neighbor."

"Pffsh," Patrick scoffed.

"Did he…touch you? I mean Arthur?"

"Mr. Dale, Mr. Dale did what Mr. Dale does. And that information doesn't need to be made public to Arthur, you hear me?

"Why not? I firmly believe it's what caused you."

"What caused me?! You have no clue about me. But you will."

Under normal circumstances, Dr. Benson would have kept on probing, but these weren't normal circumstances. Patrick could explode at any time. He thought it best to close it off.

"One more question. Can you please stop killing my staff?"

"I'd like to say I would…but it's so much fun. I've had my eye on Gladys…"

Dr. Benson shot up from his posture with a sad look on his face. "Please, Patrick, please don't kill her. Just let me help you. I can help you. You don't have to do this."

"I know that Dr. Benson, but I love doing it. It's what I know. Have you told the sun not to rise? Have you told the fish not to swim? To ask me not to do this would be the same thing."

Tears started flowing down Dr. Benson's face as Patrick just looked at him and smiled.

"You poor thing, Dr. Benson. Look at you. You have no purpose in life. You're miserable."

"And what's your purpose? Terror? You asshole!"

"Get mad, Dr. Benson, that's the spirit. But the truth is that the world is a lot lonelier than it looks. Everyone is looking for someone or something, their purpose in life."

"And what are you looking for?"

"Now that I've found you, nothing," Patrick said, smiling.

After his smile subsided, Patrick just looked deeply into nothing. As if he was looking through stuff instead of at it. Finally, after moments of silence, he opened back up.

"Enough talk about me for now. There'll be more time for that later."

The only reassuring part of that sentence was that Dr. Benson knew he would be alive for a little bit longer. He didn't know what he feared more, his passion for little boys being known or being killed by Patrick.

"Tell me about Tommy. How did you two pick him? The truth, Dr. Benson."

Dr. Benson sniffled and looked up from his downtrodden position.

"I have…I have a sickness."

"No, tell me your process. Why him? From the beginning."

"Well, I knew Mayor Jenkins from upstate New York. There were these clubs up there. Clubs for guys like Jenkins and I. These clubs were full of influential people. You wouldn't believe it. There were Senators, wealthy people, even some celebrities. It was very exclusive. Don Jenkins and I hit it off right away. We became pretty good friends. I was trying to make it onto the psychiatry scene with something big. He moved out here and started doing some good work. He phoned me and told me about this funding he put in for to build a new psychiatric hospital and he wanted me to get involved and run it."

"You see, Dr. Benson, doesn't it feel good to let it all out?"

"Stop fuckin' with me, Patrick."

"Ha, ha, ha," he laughed sadistically. "Then what?"

"I moved over here, and we picked up where we left off in New York. Don set up a school day where the kids would come to city hall and meet with the various professionals there so they could see different careers. He did this every year for the fifth graders. We had a fresh supply of boys all the time."

"How did you pick Tommy?"

"Tommy wasn't the first. He's just the one you know about. There were some before him and some after."

"I don't doubt that for a second. Just like there were some before Martin, and there will be some after. So how?"

Patrick was pushing for the answer of how they picked Tommy. He admired the art of stalking and taking the prey.

"Don would get the boys one-on-one and just chat with them. Tommy's dad passed, and his mom was a bit of a shut in. It really messed up Tommy when his father died. It wasn't hard for the mayor to use his power over him. Tommy got to liking the attention after a while. I guess you get used to it."

"You're no different than me, Dr. Benson. You found the weak ones. You found the ones that you could play around with, with no repercussions. You're sick, you know that?"

"I know," Dr. Benson said crying.

"Well, we've made real progress here. Anything else you want to add?" Patrick said calmly.

"Word got leaked about the last killing. The town is riled up again. The mayor is going to hold a town hall meeting to talk with the people. Please stop, Patrick. Please, no more bodies. At least not any from the hospital."

"I have a good thing going, Dr. Benson. I have a warm bed to sleep in, and I can kill whomever I want without any consequences. You want me just to give that up?"

"At least stop killing my staff."

"Oh, so it's okay as long as it doesn't affect you?"

"That's not what I meant. I meant the Chief of Police and a detective are starting to think something is wrong. And the killing patterns match yours. Something is going to give. The Chief said something about the feds coming out here. You don't want that."

Dr. Benson waited for confirmation of his request, but he didn't get any. His initial strategy to plead with Patrick didn't work. Patrick was too smart for psychological tactics, so Dr. Benson had to try anything else at his disposal.

"Sleep well, Dr. Benson."

"Yeah," was the only thing Dr. Benson could think of to say back.

After the room had gone quiet and cold, Dr. Benson turned off the light and slid under the blankets like a child scared of the boogeyman. The analogy wasn't too far off. There was a definite difference when talking to Arthur and Patrick. Dr. Benson felt a softness and maybe even a kind way about Arthur, but Patrick was dark. The way his eyes looked, the way his voice deepened, the difference was clear. One you could have a beer with, the other was not to be messed with.

Dr. Benson never slept on the nights when Patrick came to visit him. He mostly just lay there, paralyzed with fear. So far that hadn't done anything for him. He would have to adapt. He would have to change. He would have to go from prey to predator, but he would have to be careful. Patrick was cunning

and smart, but he was limited on resources; Dr.
Benson wasn't. He spent the rest of the night
counting the metaphorical weapons he had at his
disposal. He was down, but he wasn't out.

TWENTY-ONE

"It wasn't as dark and scary as it sounds. I had a lot of fun...killing somebody's a funny experience."

-Albert DeSalvo "The Boston Strangler; 13 victims; Chelsea, Massachusetts USA

"This is Dr. Benson," he said, picking up the telephone.

"Harold. Don here. How are you?"

"Good, Don. What's going on?"

Dr. Benson was in his office putting the finishing touches on the profile of the Jimmy and Martin murderer.

"How's that little problem we talked about?" Jenkins asked.

"I'm handling it. I'm looking to wrap it up. It's going to take time."

"Good. I'm glad to hear that, Harold. Listen, I'm having a town hall meeting, and I'd like for you to be there. The people are concerned, and rightly so. It might help calm them down to hear from the doctor who has Arthur Fritz in his care."

"What do you want me to tell them, Don? I mean, New Hope has a killer on their hands. Do you expect me to lie?"

"Now, I'm not asking you to lie. I'm asking you to tell them that Arthur is safe and secure. They are really worked up that he might still be doing this stuff. All those bodies and the way they were killed are still fresh in people's minds. I need you on this one."

"Okay. I'll do it."

"Good. Tomorrow at five p.m. Be there a little early, I want to talk to you about something else."

"See you there, Don."

★★★★★★★★★★

Dr. Benson showed up early just as instructed. He parked in the back and took the rear entrance into city hall. Crowds were already starting to gather out in the front. Dr. Benson wasn't prepared for any of this. Now he was going to be standing directly in front of an angry mob who saw the authority standing in the front as part of the problem and not part of the solution. New Hope was barely healing from the work of a madman, one they thought they had captured. It was understandable why they felt the way they did. The part they didn't know was that Dr. Benson was tied into all of this. He wasn't guilty of any of the previous killings, but he definitely had a hand in the others. Now he had to put on his acting face to tell everyone that everything was going to be okay.

"Harold!" Jenkins yelled from down the hallway.

Dr. Benson didn't feel like being loud, so he just waved in acknowledgment. Don Jenkins waved him into his office. Dr. Benson trotted down the hallway and into the Mayor's office. Jenkins was dressed up as usual with his tie pinned down and matching cufflinks. Even if he weren't in control, he would at least look like he was.

"Don. How are you?"

"I'm good. Thanks for coming. Chief Nelson will be here in a few minutes, and we can talk about what we're going to say."

Jenkins stood up and walked over to his window that was facing toward the town square. He put his hands on his waist and looked stoically out on his city.

"What did you need to talk to me about, Don?" Dr. Benson asked.

The mayor turned around slowly with a crooked smile on his face, the kind that Dr. Benson knew all about.

"I have this kid, Bobby Harris."

"No! No more, Don!"

"Oh, don't you get all high and fuckin' mighty on me now. I know you can't resist them anyway. I'm talking about some Grade-A ass here Harold. Like the kind in New York. I..."

"Just stop it. I don't want anything to do with this one."

Jenkins had a look on his face as if he had been betrayed by his best friend and, in a sense, he had.

"Harold, you aren't quitting on me, are you? You've eaten the forbidden fruit, and nothing will ever taste the same again. So, don't you back out on me now! Does this have anything to do with whoever knows about Tommy?"

Dr. Benson couldn't look Jenkins in the eyes. His poker face was shit, and he knew Jenkins would know he was lying. But it didn't matter, he knew anyway.

"Dammit, Harold. You're putting me in a bad spot here. You know damn well I can take care of this situation if need be. But you have to tell me."

"Trust me when I say you can't help me, Don. Let me handle this one. You aren't in any danger right now. I'll let you know if it ever gets there, but I'm certain it won't. I have a plan."

He didn't really have a plan, but he would get one soon. Don didn't need to know that, he just needed to know it was under control and he needed Chief Nelson off his back. There was the illusion again that haunted Dr. Benson his whole life: control. He was further from that than he'd ever been, but that was the great trick. It made him believe he was still in control. Like the devil making people believe he didn't exist, such was the case with control.

"You know what? You can help me, Don."

Jenkins swung around from the window and looked back at Dr. Benson. "Oh yeah? What's that?"

"You can get the Chief and Detective Reynolds off my back. Arthur has nothing to do with these new killings. They keep pushing for answers, and they keep bugging me about it."

"Okay. I can do that. But it was my idea that it could be him. I was putting a lot of pressure on them. I may have suggested it. I'm sorry. I'll get them off your case."

"Thank you. Are we good here?" Dr. Benson asked.

"No, about the other matter with Bobby Harris. The offer still stands."

"Dammit, Don. I shouldn't."

"Hey. You don't have to feel bad about it. This has been going on as long as man has been around. Hell, the Romans did it! Greatest civilization that ever ruled."

"That doesn't make it right, Don. We both know it's wrong."

"Suit yourself, Harold. But if you change your mind, you know who to call."

"Yeah, we'll see."

Dr. Benson's weakness was eating at him like never before. Patrick was right about vices. Now Dr. Benson could relate, in a strange and foreign way, to Patrick's need to kill. He could understand the insect that clawed at him from the inside, an itch that must be scratched. Was Patrick getting to him?

The very courtroom where Arthur Fritz was tried and found guilty of being criminally insane was where the town hall meeting was to take place. It was ironic that Arthur was the one still causing chaos and fear to run rampant after he was found to be criminally insane. That was how easy it was to trick the people who were asleep. That was how a wolf could walk amongst sheep and never be seen. It's not as if the sheep were blind, they merely had their eyes closed.

Grumbling and small, isolated conversations were going on all at once, and the discord was echoing against the stale courtroom walls. All the seats along the wooden benches were filled, and people were standing up against the sides and back as well. It wasn't quite as full as during the trial, but it was close. Angst and confusion were the attire for the evening. It was even more apparent when the Chief of Police, the Mayor of New Hope, and an up-and-coming psychiatrist walked in through the judge's chamber in the back.

"Good evening, everyone!" Mayor Jenkins said in his deep and commanding voice.

He gave it a few seconds so that the murmurs would stop before he started again. "Thank you all for coming. I know this is a scary time for our lovely community. I…"

"Scary, hell! We're terrified, goddammit!" an older man interrupted.

Cheers and yells started in a chain reaction. Mayor Jenkins put his hands in the air as to calm the mob, and it worked.

"As I was saying, I've asked Chief Nelson and Dr. Harold Benson to come up here with me and answer any questions you might have. We are here to assure you that we are doing all we can, and if we need to, we can call in reinforcements from down in D.C. So, please, raise your hands, and we can get to your questions one at a time. We'll stay out here all night if we have to. Thank you."

Hands began to shoot out across the crowd, and Mayor Jenkins pointed to the first one that caught his eye.

"You. Go ahead," Jenkins barked.

The middle-aged man stood up and cleared his throat. "Hi, I'm Bob Childress. I live up north on a farm with my family. I just wanted to know what leads you have. Do you have any suspects? Thank you."

"I'm going to defer this question to Chief Nelson," Mayor Jenkins said.

"Thank you, Bob. Yes, we are working up a profile with Dr. Benson here. So far, there have only been two murders. Both were young men that worked up at the new hospital. Right now, we don't have any suspects, but we are aggressively tracking clues and leads."

Whispers rang out again at the mention of zero leads when another man in the back stood up.

"If I catch that son of a bitch in my house or on my property I'm gonna kill the bastard!"

"Now, listen folks, we don't need any vigilantes out here running around. You are within your legal rights to protect yourself and your family, but you need to be careful. The way to really protect yourself is for you to be aware. Don't be out late at night alone. Don't be wandering around after dark. Keep your doors and windows locked. If you see something suspicious, you need to call the police department immediately."

"Dammit, Nelson! We ain't never had to lock our doors before that damn Arthur started killing people. Now we have to live in fear! Is he back!?" another man yelled out.

The crowd looked on intently, waiting for the answer to the real question they all wanted to ask. Dr. Benson stepped forward to field the question while adjusting the glasses on his face. The crowd went silent.

"First of all, Arthur Fritz is in lockdown, and he is receiving treatment. He is heavily medicated and is being monitored twenty-four hours a day. Arthur Fritz is not out killing people again. Don't believe the sewing circle talk and rumors. Secondly, I'm working with Chief Nelson, and I've made a preliminary profile based on the reports. This appears to be the work of a zealous fanatic. He is apparently targeting members of my staff in order to appear to help Arthur Fritz. It is his way of showing allegiance to him. Or to give him praise, in other words. This fanatic is sloppy and will get caught. He has left the crime scenes with lots of clues, but those clues take time to analyze and work. This guy seems to be an opportunist, so as Chief Nelson said, be vigilant out there and stay in groups. Thank you."

Mayor Jenkins and Chief Nelson entertained some questions from the crowd while Dr. Benson stood quietly in the background. Amidst all the commotion, he was formulating how to stop Patrick from killing people in the town, but more importantly, stop Patrick from killing him. The man's outburst from earlier gave Dr. Benson an idea. If he caught the killer in his house, he was within his legal rights to protect himself. He could show that Arthur had keys to all the doors and was letting himself out and killing people. It might be a slight, professional black eye for himself, but that was a small price to pay for getting rid of the biggest pain in his ass. It would be an even better story than he could imagine. The only puzzle piece he had to account for was whatever evidence Patrick had and where he kept it. While it wasn't a one hundred percent developed plan, it was a start. He could also never forget how unpredictable Patrick was. One night he was pleasant, the next he could cut Dr. Benson's face with the same knife he used to cut his steaks up with. Patrick was sly and ruthless and always a step ahead. Dr. Benson would have to be smart about this one. A small smile crept across his face as the angry crowd chanted and clamored on their way out of the courtroom.

TWENTY-TWO

"Hey, fellas! How about this for a headline for tomorrow's paper? 'French Fries."

-James French; 2 victims; Oklahoma City, Oklahoma USA

A few days had passed since the town hall meeting. Things seemed normal for a brief period. Arthur had been quietly hanging out in the rec room with Old George. The town had started to feel a little better. Even Dr. Benson was cautiously optimistic about this debacle being put to bed, but it was still mostly unrest. He had been around enough crazy people to know and understand that rarely do things stay calm for long.

Dr. Benson walked casually down the main hallway on the first floor, whistling a tune that had somehow got stuck in his head. This was the calm before the storm, and Dr. Benson was doing what he could to figuratively batten down the hatches. He made his way to the door marked "Supplies. Staff members only." He slid his master key and looked around before unlocking the door. Not that he didn't have permission to be in there, but when someone is doing something wrong, it's hard not to look guilty. Inside were the usual basic hospital supplies. Rolls of gauze and stacks of linen lined the wall to his left. To his right was a hanger rack with orderly uniforms and operating uniforms for when the other doctors performed lobotomies and electroshock therapy sessions. Inside the main room was another locked door that only a few staff members had access to. Dr. Benson easily moved into the next room where medical equipment, scalpels, and the powerful drugs were kept, not the ones dispersed to patients, but the ones used to subdue them. This was the very reason that Dr. Benson was in there in the first place. He was looking for Etorphine, a synthetic opioid that was developed a few years back. It was originally created to take down elephants and large rhinos, but with the latitude given to doctors and the lack of laws governing mentally ill patients, it was gaining popularity in mental institutions as a quick way to neutralize a rabid and neurotic patient. Dr. Benson fumbled and flipped through the vials until he found the one he was looking for.

Dr. Benson was overjoyed and felt his control coming back that he couldn't help but sing aloud to a jingle he heard on the radio a few days back. It was a popular product jingle that was making its way around the tv and radio waves.

"Oh Fab, they put, real borax in you!

"Oh Fab, they put, real borax in you!

"It's a new kind of clean! You'll want to get close to!

"Oh Fab, I'm glad, they put real borax in you!"

He sang the words aloud and smiled as he held the vial upside down and stuck the needle in. He slowly pulled back on the syringe, drawing the clear liquid in slowly until it had 4ccs…more than enough to calm Patrick down.

"Oh Fab, they put, real borax in you!

"Oh Fab, they put, real borax in you," He sang, finally trailing off to a low-level hum.

"That's right you fuckin' crazy bastard. I'll be putting some REAL Etorphine in you! Lights out, Patrick," Dr. Benson said with an evil grin that could rival Patrick's.

★★★★★★★★★★

Back in Dr. Benson's office, he sat gingerly in his chair and pulled an old memo pad from the bottom drawer. After putting the Etorphine in his coat, he flipped through the memo until he stopped at a number and began to dial.

"Clyde? This is Harold. Harold Benson."

Clyde was an old colleague of Dr. Benson from New York. They were roommates in college and even worked at the same hospital during their residency. While their paths differed after that first job, they always remained friends.

"Dr. Benson! I should say the famous Dr. Benson! Hello, old friend. How are you?"

"I'm well, thank you. How is New York?"

"I tell you, this city is really moving, not like it was in upper New York."

"Listen, I'm pressed for time, and I need your help."

"Sure, we go back a long way. What can I do for you, Harold?"

"I need you to look up someone in your old files for me. Arthur Fritz. It would be somewhere up in Essex County. Can you do that for me?"

"Of course. If I find something, I'll call you right away."

"Right away, Clyde. It's imperative."

"You got it."

"I've got to run. I'll be expecting your call."

★★★★★★★★★★

Dr. Benson didn't know when Patrick would be over next, but it didn't matter. He had to figure out where the evidence of Tommy B. was stashed first. Besides, it wouldn't be easy to get Patrick that close to him. Dr. Benson felt that if Patrick were ever that close to him, it would be to harm him physically. The psychological damage he could do from a distance. In either case, Dr. Benson had to be ready.

Dr. Benson took off from work early that day with the Etorphine in tow. He had an appointment with a door and window specialist. Not that changing the locks or beefing up security would help keep Patrick out, but it would keep Patrick from suspecting that Dr. Benson was giving in to him and wanted him in the house. It would keep him off the trail of his plans. He needed any advantage he could get now.

"Well, Harold..."

"Please, call me Dr. Benson."

The locksmith looked at him a little strangely, but it was all part of Dr. Benson gaining his control back.

"Yeah. Sorry, Dr. Benson. We upgraded all the locks on your doors. We fortified them with deadbolts. Makes it very secure that way. We also put in new locks in all the windows. They aren't getting in here unless they break the windows."

"Thank you. It makes me feel safer. And here is your check."

Dr. Benson handed the man a check, and they shook hands. Dr. Benson quietly shut the door behind him and started fumbling with his new keys and began to replace the old ones on his keyring. After putting the new keys on, he hurried over to his room. Dr. Benson frantically started looking for a place to put the syringe of Etorphine.

"Think. Think. You're going to need it quickly."

Dr. Benson positioned himself on top of his neatly made bed to simulate his reach. He placed it under the mattress and laid on his back while quickly trying to grab it, making a stabbing gesture with it in the air.

"Too slow," he said shaking his head.

"Ah-ha!"

He laid the syringe on his nightstand and ran to his study where he grabbed a piece of tape. He ran back into the bedroom and carefully taped the syringe behind his headboard just at shoulder level as if he was sitting up. This was normally the position he was in when Patrick was there. Sitting back up straight, he practiced reaching for it by bringing his left arm directly to the left of his face. His hands landed on it perfectly, and he easily ripped it off.

"There we go."

Over and over he practiced until it was all reflex instead of thought. After not having had a drink in a few weeks, he walked into the living room and filled his glass with bourbon. Dr. Benson was proud. For a second, he was having fun, matching wits against the criminally insane, yet genius prowess of Patrick Leopold.

★★★★★★★★★★

Dr. Benson wasn't necessarily expecting Patrick that night, but he wouldn't have been surprised if he had shown up. Without warning, and at nearly one in the morning, Dr. Benson woke to a loud crash of glass at the back door. Adrenaline pumped into Dr. Benson's veins, and he sat up straight in his bed, just like he practiced to get into his position. A faint click could be heard and then footsteps along the floor. Whoever it was, wasn't trying to hide the fact that they were in his house. The footsteps continued until they reached the entrance to the bedroom. There they stopped and Dr. Benson finally and reluctantly clicked on the light. Sure enough, it was Patrick.

"Changing the locks on me, Dr. Benson?"

"Yes, well…"

"That's a thing of beauty between us. We both rely on being tacticians and crafty in our every move, but when the situation calls for it, such as you changing the locks, I can turn into the raging animal with no remorse that you think I am. I can move away from the precision moves and rely on brute force to accomplish my mission. Can you?" Patrick said, taking his seat in the corner.

Dr. Benson's heart was beating through his chest. He didn't know if Patrick would be upset by this and come near him. He had practiced his move many times but was still shaking at the thought of having to do it.

"Dr. Benson, you're shaking like a leaf. I have to believe it isn't me. We've gotten to know each other quite well. So, what is it? What are you hiding? Oh, are you just scared that the whole door thing would piss me off?" Patrick began to laugh in his maniacal form once again. "Oh, Dr. Benson, you make me laugh."

"Why?"

"Because you change all the locks and I just smash through the window like a hungry Neanderthal. And now you're shaking because you think I'm going to hurt you for that. Typical Pavlovian response, the same way that a child thinks they are in trouble when they've spilled a glass of milk on the floor. Kids are going to make messes. Any reasonable parent knows that. And any reasonable doctor knows that a psychopath is going to break a few things in his path too. Does that sound about right?"

Dr. Benson kept playing the scared game so that Patrick felt he had the control. And Dr. Benson wasn't exactly playing it. He was genuinely scared, he just didn't have to hide it now.

"So, what are we going to talk about tonight?" Dr. Benson asked.

"You know, I really like the format of our last session. You ask me questions about me, and then we talk about you. How does that sound?"

"It sounds good. You seem to be in a cheery mood tonight."

"Yes, well they served roast beef for dinner tonight. I guess the taste of rare meat on my tongue and the look of a bloody plate after just got me excited and put me in the mood."

"In the mood for what?"

"More blood, and more meat," Patrick said smiling.

That didn't make Dr. Benson feel any better. He knew that Patrick could just go off his rails at any time. After all, violence was his thing. It was all serial killers' thing.

"So, go ahead," Patrick said with his hands calmly in his lap.

"I don't know where to start. I guess I could start by saying the town is up in arms again. They think there is a new killer on the loose. I'm sure you just love that feeling, don't you?"

"Of course, I do."

"Tell me, Patrick. Why do you kill? Really, why? What do you get out of it?"

Patrick sat back to think of the answer to the question. It was a good one, and he could tell that Dr. Benson wanted a deeper answer instead of the generic one.

"Well, Dr. Benson, I think of it like this: nature is always moving into chaos. Things naturally go from a state of order to disorder. Take your yard for example. I could see that you made your last mow before the winter. If you were never to touch your lawn for five years, you would see that it would get overgrown and eventually take over your house. All these structures and things of order that man makes, they need upkeeping. They need maintenance to stay looking so lovely. But you are putting energy into something that is temporary. I guess for me it feels natural to tear apart a human body, something that is most definitely a thing of order and structure. I love to watch the blood run like a river. Its natural state is to decay and return to the earth. It feels good to give the universe what it wants, which is more chaos, more disorder."

"But doesn't it feel good to look at a well-kept flower garden? Or maybe a beautiful structure? Like the Empire State Building or the Statue of Liberty? Don't those make you happy?" Dr. Benson asked.

"Happiness? We will do anything to make ourselves our happy. We even lie to get it done."

"Are you going to keep killing people? This has to come to an end, Patrick. You can't just keep killing people."

"Why can't I?"

"Well, you'll run out of people, for one."

"And that's a bad thing?"

"Yes, Patrick. That's a horrible thing. You know that."

Patrick just laughed again. He couldn't be reasoned with. He was aware that he was insane. He was aware that what he did was wrong and he did it anyway. There would be no dealing with him in any conventional manner. Dr. Benson was ready to make his move, he just wasn't willing to make it tonight. He thought about provoking Patrick into getting close to him but decided against it. Patrick was in a good mood this evening, maybe he should just keep it that way.

"Patrick, there is another matter I want to discuss with you. The hospital has an inspection and a compliance audit coming up next week. There will be a lot of doctors who are going to be interested in seeing your progress, or rather, Arthur's. They will be interested in talking to you."

"And what leverage do you think you have over me to play nice?"

"I don't have any Patrick, just hope."

"I'll be honest. My initial thought was to turn your office into the wild fucking west. And when I run out of bullets, I'll bite their faces off. Blood will be spilled everywhere."

Without reacting too much, Dr. Benson remained calm and asked a follow-up question. "What was your second thought?"

"Maybe just let Arthur deal with that shit. I'm not a very social person. I like my privacy."

"Can I count on Arthur being there?"

"You can't count on anything with me, Dr. Benson, but we'll see."

TWENTY-THREE

"I always had a desire to inflict pain on others and to have others inflict pain on me. The desire to inflict pain, that is all that is uppermost."

-Albert Fish; at least 6 victims; Washington D.C. USA

Dr. Benson had decided to repair the window to the back door, but from now on, he was going to leave it unlocked. Unless he was living in a cave with a three-foot-thick reinforced wall at the entrance, he wasn't going to keep Patrick out. Even then, he might still get in. October was here, and the chill from the north had begun to make its way down and into New Hope. Winters always started early that high north and lasted well into April.

October meant a new fiscal year in government terms. That also meant a new round of funding for the hospital. The team from D.C. was here to discuss old projects that needed to be finished, as well as new ones from the original proposal. Word of Dr. Benson's cleanly run hospital had reached down the entire east coast. There was even talk of bringing new patients from overcrowded facilities all over the country. Mayor Jenkins had made sure that Dr. Benson got the attention and recognition he deserved. All the expansion and growth was all right, but Dr. Benson had only one major concern, Patrick showing up. He did, after all, still have his six-shot revolver. Dr. Benson wasn't feeling comfortable, but he didn't have much of a choice: Patrick was in charge.

★★★★★★★★★★

"Welcome! As you know, my name is Dr. Harold Benson," Dr. Benson said with a smile.

Dr. Benson stood with Gladys by his side at the front of the cafeteria table, both wearing larger-than-usual smiles. The group he was talking to was a bunch of overdressed committee members who held the purse strings. Most of them were doctors, but a few were politicians from various counties in New York. All were part of the boards and committees. Every year the group got a little larger, and this year it was the biggest yet. Some of it could be attributed to the vast empire Dr. Benson was building, but most of it was from the notoriety of Arthur Fritz. Only staff members were allowed into the building and visitors were never allowed into any restricted areas. These people took full advantage of getting on the inspection team to meet Arthur in person.

"If you need anything, coffee, water, please let any of us know. This is my Chief of Personnel, Gladys Johnston. She will be taking those of you interested in our records management and federal forms processing down to where we keep those. The rest of you will come with me, and we will tour the facility and some of the improvement projects that you are well aware of by now. Are there any questions?"

A hand shot up in the front. "We would like to see Arthur Fritz and discuss some of the things you've been doing with him."

"Of course, there is plenty of time for all that," Dr. Benson said hesitantly.

He knew deep down they were going to ask to see him, but he hoped it wouldn't be with as much enthusiasm as his fellow doctor had. It made him feel that Arthur was the only reason for this visit. If they came out unscathed by Patrick, everything would be okay. Leaving with the funding he asked for would be icing on the cake.

Dr. Benson led the remainder of the group down the east wing and down into the rec room. He could tell by their faces they didn't really give a shit about anything he was showing them. He knew what they really wanted.

"Okay, folks. If you follow me this way, I'm going to show you the basement, and then we'll go have a talk with Arthur."

A wave of relief washed over the doctors when they heard the words. Dr. Benson and the group went down the stairwell and into the basement. The damp and musky smell was still there, but this time it was properly lit and didn't present an ominous feeling.

"That there is the boiler room. As you can tell, it's quite humid down here. We are looking at getting some better ventilation. That should clear up that little problem. This room back here is where we do some experimental sciences with electroshock therapy and full-frontal lobotomies."

Dr. Benson swung the double doors open, and the room was sterile and clean. Green and white tiles lined the floor. Toward the back of the room was an operating table with large lights coming down

from the ceiling. In the left of the room was a chair
that closely resembled an electric chair. It had old
leather restraints dangling from the arm rests and leg
paneling.

"Dr. Benson, how many lobotomies have
you or your team performed since opening?" one of
the doctors asked.

"Good question."

Dr. Benson thought back to his conversation
with Patrick where he didn't know the exact number
of little boys he had violated. Was Patrick right? At
least in the professional sense, Patrick knew exactly
how many people he had killed.

"We have performed three since opening
our doors. One of them was a volatile young man
who was later transferred back to New York.
Another later died as a result of the procedure, and
the third currently resides here in our facility. He is
doing well and seems to be no bother to anyone
anymore. It's quite a useful tool."

"Thank you, Dr. Benson. One more
question."

"Sure."

"Have you thought about lobotomy as an
option for Arthur Fritz?"

Dr. Benson walked from the cabinet with
medical tools, saws, and knives in it to look the
group in the eye.

"I think Arthur can be helped with
conventional medicine. He has a deeply split persona
that is very aggressive and very dangerous. If we can

get to and treat that, then there may be no use for such harsh treatment. However, if this persona continues in any capacity to be a harm to himself or others, then there may not be any alternatives. You see, as doctors in this field of medicine, we must do what is right by the patient, no matter how criminal they are. But in this case, Arthur Fritz needs more time to see if he is responding to the medicine. He is under careful watch, and I meet with him at least twice a week. He is a rather calm and mild individual, as I think you will soon see when you meet him."

"Umm, Dr. Benson?" another hand shot up from the group.

"Yes?"

"Have you met with or talked to his other personality?"

The others all turned their attention back to Dr. Benson. It was as if he had asked the question for the rest of them.

"So far, I have spoken with him once. He is a very, very deeply disturbed man. He is obsessed with killing and knows that it is wrong, which makes it even more challenging. But, we are early in our treatment with Arthur. We have much to explore, and many new therapies are becoming available at our disposal."

"Is there any way to tell which persona you are dealing with? And could there be more than two?"

"Great question."

Dr. Benson paused before answering as not to give too much away. Patrick said he didn't like these types of things, but one never knew with him. He could show up at any time and crash the party. Not to mention, he had a revolver that he most likely carried on himself.

"There are no distinguishing features as far as I can tell. It is mostly in the manner in which he talks. The other persona is named Patrick, and he is very eager to tell you who he is."

The group nodded as if to be very happy with what Dr. Benson was doing in here.

"Enough of the tour. Let us go talk to Arthur."

Dr. Benson grabbed the phone on the wall and rang up Doug. "Hello, this is Dr. Benson. Please get Gladys and bring Arthur up to my office. Yes. Full shackles. Thank you."

"Okay, gentlemen, my staff will have Arthur up there shortly. Now is a good time to use the facilities and take a smoke break if needed."

Dr. Benson nervously opened his office door to find Gladys, Doug, and Arthur. Arthur was shackled to the chair that was bolted to the ground, and Gladys stood directly to his left, hand in her pocket and fingers on the Etorphine. The moment had come. It was now or never. Dr. Benson's career was hanging in the balance. It was looking directly at him, shackled into a cold, metal chair.

"Gentlemen, this is Mr. Arthur Fritz. Arthur, these men are with the government. They provide the funding for our hospital."

Dr. Benson spoke in tones as if Arthur was some freak show on display. All the doctors looked on as they lined up around the sides of Arthur, keeping a safe distance.

"Gladys, Doug, thank you. You may step out now."

"Arthur, let me introduce you. From left to right here is Dr. Larry Howard, Dr. Steven Yang, Dr. Barry Lervis, Dr. Jacob Parvin and Dr. Ronald Neiman."

Dr. Benson purposely used the first names so he could tell whom exactly he was dealing with. The team of doctors stared and studied Arthur. Dr. Benson snuck behind his desk and caught a one-on-one glimpse of Arthur. Arthur's doe-eyed and subtle blank stare suddenly went sharp. Dr. Benson's eyebrows tightened as if trying to read Arthur's face. Suddenly, Arthur winked his right eye at Dr. Benson.

Dr. Jacob Parvin moved around from the side and up in front of Arthur.

"Hello, Arthur. My name is Jacob. I wanted to ask you a few questions."

"Sure Dr. Parvin. Ask away…"

A cold sweat came over Dr. Benson. In an instant, he knew he wasn't dealing with the calm and likable Arthur. He was now dealing with the cold and calculating Patrick, who most likely had a revolver tucked into his underwear.

"Tell me about your treatment here?"

"Oh, Dr. Benson is just the greatest you know? He treats me well. As if I was a young boy, learning from him."

Dr. Jacob Parvin nodded his head in agreement. Patrick just smiled like a smart-ass kid who knew he was pissing off his parents.

"And how do you like the facility?"

"I just love it here," Patrick replied.

"Well you certainly seem like you're in a chipper mood today, Arthur," Dr. Parvin remarked.

"Yes, well, I feel like a young schoolboy, innocent and fresh."

"Thank you, Arthur!" Dr. Benson interrupted, with a slightly red face.

"No, thank *you*, Dr. Benson. Thank you for letting me meet all those wonderful doctors. So many doctors. Six to be exact, including you. What a great round number."

"Yes, excellent observation Pa...Arthur," Dr. Benson said, quickly trying to change the subject.

Dr. Benson knew that Patrick had the six-shot revolver in his pants, and there was nothing he could do about it. He didn't know if Patrick was just going to sit there and mentally torture him or if he was, in fact, going to turn this place into the wild fuckin' West as Patrick had stated earlier. Neither outcome would surprise him, but as a psychiatrist, Dr. Benson knew that at this moment, he could only control himself. And if he were honest with himself, he would admit that he was drained and exhausted from playing these games with Patrick. He was tired of carting around tons of guilt. Wasted from knowing that at any moment his dark secret could be exposed. Having to choose between the weakness and cravings of his ego and the public knowing the truth tore at him. Like trying to serve two masters, he'd never win.

Still shackled to the chair, Patrick sat still with a coy and crooked smile. He did his time as some sideshow. He even answered questions politely and didn't embarrass Dr. Benson any further. Waiting a few more minutes, Dr. Benson stepped outside and called on Gladys and Doug to come take Arthur back to his cell. After Arthur had left, the group broke apart from a little huddle in the corner.

"Well, Dr. Benson, you certainly run a tight ship here and seem to have everything under control," one of the doctors said.

"Yes, we are very impressed. We will get back with you on any issues, but for now, consider your funding secure and intact."

"Why, thank you very much. I appreciate you all coming out and taking the time."

After the room had been cleared, Dr. Benson let out a sigh of relief. He had dodged a figurative and literal bullet on this one, making his plan seem more and more sustainable by the day. Everything was in place, and he was very confident things would end soon. All he needed was Patrick to get close enough to him to sedate him with the Etorphine. Then Dr. Benson could stage a break in and kill Patrick with the revolver, a knife or whatever method he chose. Maybe he would make it slow for all the pain and heartache that Patrick had caused him. Maybe he would just put a bullet in his head and move on with his life. That kind of ending would certainly add some excitement to his book and a hero aspect to his life. Yes, things were going his way. One step at a time.

TWENTY-FOUR

"She isn't missing. She's at the farm right now."

-Ed Gein; 2 victims; La Crosse County, Wisconsin USA

"Patrick?" Dr. Benson cried out in the dark.

Tiny slivers of moonlight moved through the shades. In any normal circumstance, the shadows would have been Cornelius knocking something over in the kitchen or just playing with the pull switch on the lamp. But it took Dr. Benson a few seconds to realize that this wasn't an ordinary circumstance and that it was mostly the demented, split personality of Arthur Fritz.

"I feel like we've made progress in our relationship, Dr. Benson. I don't feel the need to sneak in anymore, you immediately know who's here."

Dr. Benson yawned and quickly got into his trained position in case tonight was the night that Patrick wanted to harm him. In fact, he had been thinking of ways to agitate and anger Patrick to provoke something. Anything to get the ball rolling, as it was becoming too much of a cross to bear.

"Thank you for being a real asshole and showing up for the inspection, Patrick."

"Oh Dr. Benson, did my little jokes upset you?"

"Maybe. But more than anything I'm tired of you being a fuck up. Just kill me already or leave me be. You're just playing with me."

Patrick just smiled, he could tell that Dr. Benson was trying to get under his skin.

"Is that what you want? Do you really expect me to kill you?"

"Well, are you?"

"I don't know anymore, but I think so. But if you hate me now, you're going to hate me more in a few hours," Patrick said.

"Why?" Dr. Benson responded quickly.

"You asked if I am going to kill you. The answer has suddenly changed to yes."

Dr. Benson was certainly scared of Patrick, but he didn't feel like he was going to die.

"I thought you said you weren't going to do it?"

"Dr. Benson! Wake up! I have no morality! I'm as obsessed with ending lives as you are with young boys. What did you think would happen?"

Dr. Benson just shook his head in disbelief. He knew more than ever that he was going to have to make his move soon. Was it tonight? His trembling hands hoped it wasn't.

"The good news is, it's not tonight. But, we are going on a field trip. Your therapy has seemed to slow. I think that the late-night sessions might not be working anymore. You are going to grow, Dr. Benson. And with growth comes pain. Get dressed. Put on some warm clothes. We are leaving."

"What?! No!"

Patrick pulled the revolver out of his coat pocket and laid it on the dresser. "If you want it to be tonight, then we can arrange that."

"Guns aren't your style. You like to kill people slowly."

"Oh, I won't shoot you in the head, silly Dr. Benson. I'll shoot you in the gut. And then I'll peel your face off with a razor. Now, GET THE FUCK UP!"

"Okay. Okay. Relax," Dr. Benson said. He was confident that Patrick wouldn't shoot him. Then, again, he didn't know for sure.

Back in New York, in his first position in a mental hospital, they had a patient named Roger. Roger had killed his entire family in their sleep. He told them that an angel came to him one night and told him to do it. Roger was calm and sensible, and if someone didn't know he was in a hospital and had a conversation with him, they would never know he was ill. One day, three years after never hurting a fly, he suddenly lost it in the cafeteria. Roger beat another patient to death with a plastic dinner tray. When asked later why he did it, he said that he just felt the urge to kill someone. That type of acute behavior always stuck with Dr. Benson, and he always kept his guard up.

Patrick stood behind Dr. Benson while Dr. Benson took his coat off the rack and reluctantly put it on. The revolver was at Patrick's side and trained on Dr. Benson's lower back.

"So where are we going on this field trip?" Dr. Benson asked.

"You'll see soon enough. I want to show you some things. Open you up to some ideas. Educate you."

"I have plenty of education, Patrick."

"About life, yes. But not about death. You regard life as precious and make vows to extend it as far as possible, but you neglect death. Something equally important as life. Without death, there would be no life."

Dr. Benson wondered if he could have gotten back to his room quickly enough to grab the Etorphine. Tonight could very well be the night that Patrick was going to dispose of him. It might be his only chance. Without it, he was certainly dead.

"Go get the car and bring it around the front. Don't make me remind you that if you flee, the whole world will know about little Tommy B."

"What are you going to go do?" Dr. Benson asked.

Patrick paused for a second, staring at Dr. Benson. "I have to take a piss."

"Oh."

Dr. Benson pulled his Chevelle Malibu to the front of his house and waited patiently for Patrick to come out. It was a cold night, and he wondered if he should have taken his gloves. Before he could open the door and step outside, Patrick came barreling out of the front door and into the passenger seat.

"Drive."

"Where to?" Dr. Benson asked.

"Cross the old bridge and head north on Mason Road."

Dr. Benson obliged as the tires slightly peeled out on the loose gravel in his driveway. Patrick sat quietly with the gun pointed at Dr. Benson, while Dr. Benson looked cautiously at the road. Not a soul was stirring about in New Hope at this hour of the night. Not even the police would patrol, as there was usually nothing going on. The car passed over the rickety bridge before either occupant finally piped up.

"You are going to be scared tonight, but it is for your own good," Patrick said quietly.

"Please, will you tell me what's going to happen to me?"

"You'll see soon enough."

"Well, reach in the glove compartment there and get me that pack of Camels."

"I believe those things are bad for your health," Patrick said, handing him the smokes.

"Yeah, well if I'm going to die tonight, might as well enjoy one."

Dr. Benson lit one up and offered the pack to Patrick.

"No, thank you. And there you go again, making this about you. This is a field trip, Dr. Benson. Not an execution. This is for the personal growth you desperately need. And remember, with it comes the pain, I hope you can get through it."

"Fuck," Dr. Benson muttered.

"Take a right here," Patrick said, pointing toward the upcoming T in the road.

The car wound down a narrow dirt road with towering trees on both sides. The headlights did little to cut through the night while the gravel from the road popped as the tires spit it onto the underside of the car.

"Wait, Isn't this…?" Dr. Benson muttered.

"Yes, it is."

"Why are you bringing me here?"

"You want in my head, right? You want to know me? Well, you are about to learn all about me. Park right there in the front."

The car stopped slowly in front of the little wooden cabin that Arthur and Patrick used to call home. The front door of the house was boarded up and had a police sticker stapled to it.

"Wow, I only read about this place."

"Too bad we aren't going in there," Patrick replied.

Dr. Benson got out of the car and moved around to the front where Patrick was waiting. A waxing crescent moon barely provided enough light to see. The house stood ominously in front of them, dark and cold with no life emanating.

"That way," Patrick pointed with the gun.

Dr. Benson followed a small trail that led behind the house. In the darkness, he could make out a log roof that stood above the ground by no more than a foot. The narrow footpath led to the roof and to a set of stairs that met the entrance. It, too, was locked with a giant padlock and had a notice on the front.

"Now what?" Dr. Benson said.

"Here," Patrick said, handing him a key.

"Do you have a key to everything?" Dr. Benson asked.

"Everything I need to. None of this was an accident, Dr. Benson. None of this."

Dr. Benson fiddled with the key until it slid into the lock and opened with ease. Patrick pushed him forward with the muzzle of the gun. Inside it was cold and damp. Muffled sounds could be heard from the corner until Patrick pulled the string that lit up what was making the sounds.

"Oh, Patrick. What the fuck?" Dr. Benson muttered.

Little trails of minerals had formed along parts of the walls where water leaked in and ran down. Dr. Benson's words echoed in the confined room.

"Not even the screams can get out of this room," Patrick replied.

There, on the floor, was a distraught woman in her mid-forties wearing nothing but a bra and panties. Her hair was tattered and her white garments filthy from lying on the cold concrete. The restraints built into the wall held her arms securely over her head, and thick duct tape kept the screams inside her head.

"What is this?" Dr. Benson said with a frightened look.

"Not what, but who. This is Susan Buselli. You recognize the last name."

"Patrick, no."

"Yes, Dr. Benson. The first question of the night. Who is it?"

Susan's eyes followed the conversation between the two by bouncing back and forth as each talked.

"It's Tommy's mom."

"Very good. And what's going to happen to Tommy's mom tonight?"

"You're going to kill her?" A look of panic developed over Dr. Benson's face as he seemed to know this was not the correct answer.

"Wrong. You're going to kill her. You fucked her son in the ass, ruining his life. Now you are just going to finish the job. He had no father, and now he will have no mother. You are to blame for this."

Dr. Benson stood there motionless and nearly to the point of sobbing. Without warning, his instinct to take off running kicked in, and he bolted for the door. Dr. Benson was in his late fifties, and Patrick was thirty-five. Patricks' reactions were quicker than Dr. Benson's speed. Patrick lowered his shoulder and slammed into Dr. Benson's side, sending him flying into the adjacent wall and ultimately falling to the floor in nearly the same position as poor Susan Buselli. Patrick took the revolver out of his coat pocket and whipped it across Dr. Benson's face, leaving a trail of blood running down the doctor's face from the top of his eyebrow. Susan let out a filtered mumble of disgust.

Patrick kneeled so that he was eye to eye with Dr. Benson. With his index finger, Patrick interrupted the flow of blood trickling down Dr. Benson's face. Patrick held his blood-soaked finger in between them and in the light. Staring at it, he put the finger in his mouth and licked it with a slurping sound.

"Yummm."

"Patrick, don't do this. Please."

"Oh, beg, Dr. Benson. Just like Susan will in a few short minutes."

Patrick stood up and pulled out a six-inch kitchen knife that he took from Dr. Benson's kitchen. "Now get up. And kill this woman."

Dr. Benson stood up, tears flowing and sobs echoing out.

Patrick's hand extended, offering the knife to Dr. Benson. After a few moments of silence, Dr. Benson took the knife in his hand and simply stared at it.

Patrick walked over to Susan and ripped the tape off of her mouth in one quick pull.

"Ahhh!" Susan screamed.

"Shhhh. Calm down, Susan. This is the man who molested your son. He has a job to do. He has to finish fucking up young Tommy's life. You see, Dr. Benson, you are so concerned with life, that you forgot about death. You will watch Susan here transform from one to the next. And you will see that it's just as glorious as any sunrise you have ever seen."

"Please don't, Mister," Susan pleaded in between the moans. Clear snot was running from her nose and into her open mouth.

"Patrick, I can't do this," Dr. Benson said as the end of the blade shook like a leaf in the wind.

"You can, and you will do this, Dr. Benson."

"No, you can kill me. I refuse to kill her."

Susan just stared intently as they argued over her fate.

"Just take the blade and slit her throat. From here to here," Patrick gestured on his own neck.

"No. No. No."

"You fuckin' pussy! You can stick a needle in someone's head and turn them into a fuckin' vegetable without blinking an eye. You can turn Tommy into the next Patrick Leopold, but you can't finish the job! You're not a stayer, Dr. Benson! Now give me the goddamned knife!" Patrick yelled, swiping it from Dr. Benson.

In one quick motion, his outreached arm swung at poor Susan Buselli. With Patrick's right arm now behind his shoulder, like mighty Casey taking a swing, a red contour appeared on Susan's dirty neckline. She tried to scream, but only hollow bellows came out as the blood bubbled with the escaping air. Patrick turned to Dr. Benson and grabbed him forcefully behind his neck and shoved his head down to Susan's level.

"Now watch! Watch the life leave her and watch death become her. Watch!"

The gurgling became louder while Susan kicked her feet.

"The brain is confused. It can't get air. It's trying to hang on, but it can't."

Sweat was running down Patrick's temple, down the side of his cheeks and just passed his curled lips. Dr. Benson could only cry and sniffle at the bloodbath that he had just witnessed.

"This is the moment. Get closer," Patrick said, shoving their faces together.

Dr. Benson could see her pupils relaxing and contracting as they swelled and shrank from a combination of panic and loss of function.

"See it! See the life evaporating!" Patrick said as Susan's body relaxed and finally stopped moving.

"And there you have it. But you failed tonight, Dr. Benson. You failed to achieve perspective. I thought you were better than this. Maybe you'll get another chance. Or perhaps, you'll be next," he said, tossing the knife on the floor. "Let's go now. I'm tired."

TWENTY-FIVE

"It is perhaps better for the community that I should die, as it would be impossible for me to stop poisoning people."

-Anna Zanzwiger; 4 victims; Bavaria

September 10, 1967

Angie greeted me today with her usual smile. She was excited to know that I was busy having fun with my new toy. I had two rolls of film that I needed to get processed. I asked her if I could watch her do it, and she was more than happy to let me in the back. While she was quite an attractive young lady, I was still going to have to kill her. I gently flirted with her and told her that these pictures would need to be kept very discreet. She promised me she wouldn't tell a soul. I believed her, but only because I knew she wouldn't be alive.

We walked back into the darkroom, and it took a few minutes for my eyes to adjust to the dim red light. It reminded me of the red light that was installed at the New Hope Psychiatric Hospital. It glowed an eerie and uninviting red. With Arthur being the history buff that he is, I remember him telling me once about why pirates wore patches on their eyes. Me not knowing any better, I always thought it was because they played around with swords or maybe the parrots on their shoulder pecked their eyes out. Turns out it's because it keeps one eye ready for the dark when they go below deck. And when they come back up they simply switch the patch to the other eye. Brilliant!

Angie opened the canister with the exposed film. She has a delicate way about her, carefully pulling the strip out and laying it on the table. The red in her strawberry blonde hair was accented in the scarlet darkness. While she worked, she talked to me about her upbringing. Her grandparents were Irish immigrants that came here as poor as the day is long. Her parents carried on the tradition by working hard their entire lives. Angie, being more of a free spirit, went out west to see what freedom and living as a free spirit felt like. More than anything, Angie just wanted to be wanted. She expressed that by sleeping with any and all men that would have her and doing every type of drug there was. She had certainly explored her freedom until she woke to realized how the world really was and came back home to get a real job. The way hippies think really bothers me. Maybe when I'm done with this whole Dr. Benson thing, I'll head out to the west where there are plenty of people to kill. If they like to explore new things, I'll show them death in all its glory.

Angie finished the developing process and hung the pictures up to dry. She said all we had to do was wait. Angie never even looked at the pictures. I'm sure she would have said something about them if she did. It crossed my mind that she could live, but after two seconds, that answer quickly became no. No one who meets me lives. It's in my nature to kill. Even though she hadn't seen the pictures, I would kill her anyway, just for fun. She signaled for me to join her out back while the pictures dried. I followed her to the back door where she lit up a smoke and offered me a blowjob right there in the store in a seedy alley. I agreed to it. Angie flicked the barely lit cigarette and dropped to her knees. I couldn't help but think how dirty she was going to get those jeans. Just as she started to unbuckle my pants, I pulled out a Swiss Army Knife and jammed it into the top of her head. It was only a three-inch blade, and it took quite a bit of force to penetrate her thick skull. Boy, those Swiss engineers know how to make a quality product. Angie's eyes rolled back into her head while the trauma to her brain began to spread to her body. I put both of my hands around her neck and pulled her up, so her eyes were in line with mine. Her feet dangled a few inches off of the ground. The panic in eyes grew as I tightened my grip, making her lips turned blue. The struggle when a body needs oxygen is something to behold. After a minute or so I finally let go. She fell onto her back, and her hands started to convulse, and then her whole body followed. I laughed a little as I saw her laying on her back with a Swiss Army Knife sticking out of the top of her head. Even though I hear that cigarettes will kill you, it seemed wrong to let that one burn out in a slow death. I picked it up and could see her red shade of lipstick on the butt; to think that it could have been on my dick. I started to walk back into the store, and it hit me: I can't just leave her like this! That's a perfectly good knife! I can't believe I almost forgot it.

I walked back into the processing room and grabbed the photos and rest of my personal belongings.

Later that evening, I got a toasty fire going in the fireplace. It was relaxing to know that all my hard work now would pay big dividends later. After the fire had crackled and roared, I tossed all the negatives in, leaving me with only the original photos. As I scanned through the photos in the light of the fireplace, something dawned on me--I wanted a challenge, not a gimmie. I didn't want any unfair advantages over Dr. Benson, so I tossed them into the fire as well. I guess Angie didn't have to die after all. Oh well, life goes on.

—Patrick

TWENTY-SIX

"I'm a murderer, not a rapist."

*-Gary Ridgway "The Green River Killer"; 71
victims; Salt Lake City, Utah USA*

A few days had passed since the Buselli fiasco had taken place. Dr. Benson had thought about talking with Arthur, but it was no use. Arthur was clueless as to what was going on. He would just tell Dr. Benson that he was right about Patrick and that Dr. Benson should have been careful of what he wished for. But Dr. Benson was too shaken to hear the words, "I told you so." He hadn't slept in a few days, and heavy bags were starting to form under his eyes.

"I'm worried about you, Dr. Benson," Gladys said in the hallway.

"I'm fine. Just a little stressed out."

"Go home. Get some rest. Everything is fine here. We'll move some of your appointments around. Take care of yourself. You look like shit, Dr. Benson. You're falling and hitting your face on things. You have stitches above your eye for Christ's sake. And frankly, I'm worried."

"Worried about what?"

"I don't know. I've just ain't never seen you like this. It's like you're tangled up in something. It's like your mind is a million miles away."

"I'm fine, Gladys. But you're right. I need to go home. Take a Valium maybe. That little pill will help."

"Good. Now get on home. This place will be here when you get back."

Before Dr. Benson could say thank you, the phone in his office began to ring.

"I'm sorry, Gladys, but I need to take this," Dr. Benson said, scurrying away from the confrontation and into his office.

"Dr. Benson here."

"Harold. It's Clyde."

"Yes, Clyde! I've been expecting your call."

"Sorry it took so long, I had some people do a lot of digging. It looks like your famous Arthur Fritz was checked into a hospital in Essex County back when he was only nine."

"What happened?"

"The record says here, well it says here he was raped. Had some tears in his anus a few times and had to get stitches. There's nothing about who it was. Says here the family wasn't going to press charges and that he wouldn't say who did it."

"That is quite disturbing. Thank you, Clyde."

"Shall I send a copy up to you in the mail?"

"Sure. That'd be great Clyde. Thanks again. Good day."

And like that, Dr. Benson had figured out the why of Patrick. The new dilemma was that he also knew why Patrick chose him.

★★★★★★★★★★

It was barely noon when Dr. Benson dragged his tired body through the house and dropped his jacket on his chair. He stopped by his trusty bourbon bottle, put two Valiums in his mouth and downed them with a large pull from the decanter. Without even getting undressed, he crawled under his covers and pulled them over his head. All he could think about was the blood pouring out of Susan's neck, and how if poor Cornelius was there he would be purring and meowing, comforting the broken Dr. Benson. Susan's dead body bounced around in his thoughts until the drugs and booze overpowered his conscious mind and he passed out.

Dr. Benson was groggy when he finally came to. In the pitch black, he fumbled around the nightstand next to his bed until he found his glasses. Flicking on the light, he looked down at his watch to see it was a quarter past one. Upon knowing what time it was, his head darted over to the corner to see if his visitor was there. Nothing. A small wave of relief fell on him, knowing that Patrick wasn't there. But, Patrick was always there…

"Dr. Benson. Did you enjoy your drug induced sleep?" Patrick asked, standing in the doorway.

"Please, just leave me alone. I don't care anymore. You can tell everyone that I like little boys. Just leave me the fuck alone. I can't take this anymore. You killed an innocent woman."

"No, you killed her, Dr. Benson. It was your knife, with your prints on them. I was wearing gloves, remember?"

"Fuck you!" Dr. Benson said, sitting up.

Dr. Benson had to somehow get under Patrick's skin enough to get him in proximity to stick him with the syringe.

"You really are pathetic, Dr. Benson. Shall I go over there and rough you up some? Maybe you like it like that, eh? Did you hit Tommy? Or were you a sweetheart?"

"Come over here, and I'll show you."

"You're an old man. I should kill you right here and thin the herd of humanity."

"I'm not living like this for another minute. Come over and do it. I'm calling your bluff, you piece of shit!" Dr. Benson said, spitting at Patrick.

"Why, Dr. Benson, you've grown a giant pair of balls. It's about time. I thought at first that my worthy adversary would just roll over and die, but now I see you want to tussle. Well, I'll grant your wish. Let me run to the kitchen real fast."

Patrick slid out from the doorway, his footsteps could be heard from the bedroom. Dr. Benson quickly reached around the headboard and grabbed the syringe. The footsteps were growing louder and louder as he tried to hide it in the palm of his hand. Just as Patrick reached the doorway, Dr. Benson managed to get it hidden from sight.

"A good paring knife should fit just right in my hand as I carve the skin off your face. I don't generally keep trophies, but I think you'll be the exception."

Dr. Benson just sat there shivering as if he was wet and a cold breeze was hitting him. Except there was no breeze; there was only the moment of truth. Either he was going to be another victim of the insane Arthur Fritz, or he was going to be the hero who captured him the second time. He would deal with the Tommy B. blackmail thing later. First things first —subdue Patrick.

Patrick carefully and methodically stepped toward Dr. Benson, finally standing directly next to and right over him. He looked like an ordinary man, but with a small knife in his hand. He didn't appear to be as intimidating as he actually was.

"Are you ready? Are you going to fight back, or are you just going to sit there and scream?"

"I guess we'll see, won't we."

"Wow. You're not begging for your life like all the others. I'm not sure how to act," Patrick said, shifting the knife from his left hand to his right.

Patrick sunk his head down and placed the blade on Dr. Benson's cheek.

"This is going to hurt, Dr. Benson, more than you can imagine."

Dr. Benson's loose, soft skin gave way as Patrick put more pressure on the knife. Then, in one swoop, Dr. Benson yelled out and swung his fist around at Patrick.

"Ahhhhhhh!"

A low-grade moan could be heard as Patrick looked over at his shoulder to see the needle all the way in his arm. He had just enough time to look back at a wide-eyed Dr. Benson before he fell to the floor with a loud crash.

Dr. Benson looked around before laughing out loud, "Yes! You mother fucker!"

Dr. Benson was starting to show some moxie, but his victory was short-lived. He needed to tie Patrick up and get some information out of him before killing him. He needed those pictures of the mayor, Tommy and himself. He would beat Patrick unmercifully until he found them if that's what he had to do. And if Patrick wanted him to kill someone so bad then he would get a first-hand view of the action. Dr. Benson jumped out of bed and headed for his tool shed. He couldn't have planned it better, as he was already dressed from going to bed with his clothes on. Within a few minutes, he returned with a length of rope, relieved to see Patrick still laying in a pile by the bed. Grabbing Patrick by the feet, he grunted and moaned as he dragged him into the living room.

"You're going to be a sorry bastard when you wake up," Dr. Benson muttered.

Dr. Benson sat in his favorite chair, sipping on his bourbon while he waited for Patrick to come to. Finally, after a half hour, Patrick began to stir.

"Wha...?" Patrick said confused.

"Oh, good to see you, Mr. Leopold!" Dr. Benson said sarcastically.

"You sneaky fucker. I underestimated you."

Dr. Benson shifted his weight in the chair. All he could do was smile as he had finally regained control. Patrick could only talk in small amounts, as he was still groggy.

"You wanted me to kill, did you not? You wanted me to learn to take a life? Well, I'm going to take one tonight. But first, we have some business to work out," Dr. Benson said as he tapped the paring knife against his glass of bourbon.

"You don't have the stones, Dr. Benson. But I give you credit for getting me in this position."

"Tell me where you keep the evidence you have against me."

Patrick didn't respond, he just sat there, blinking his eyes and trying to focus. Dr. Benson slowly rose from the chair and walked over to Patrick.

"This is going to hurt, Patrick. More than you can imagine," Dr. Benson said, smiling and punching him in the jaw.

Patrick's head rocked from one side to the other. Dr. Benson gave him another blow on the other jaw. And another, and another, and another, until his knuckles were bleeding. Patrick didn't say a word; he just took the hits while the blood ran down from his lip.

"Where is the evidence?" Dr. Benson said, raising his fist in the air.

"Okay. Okay. No more."

"That's smart of you. I was going to use the knife next. Now, where is it?"

Patrick pointed with his face toward the shed.

"Where, goddammit?!"

"In your shed, in the box in the back corner. It's in a manila envelope."

"Good. I'll be right back. Let's see if you are lying or not. If you are, prepare yourself for the knife. And not the paring knife, the meat cleaver."

Dr. Benson returned after a short while with a large envelope in his hands. He rapped it against his legs with excitement.

"Well, well, well. It looks like the big bad Patrick is just like a bully. Hit him back, and he cowers like a beat dog," Dr. Benson said, walking around to face Patrick. "I guess I have no use for you now. Should I kill you slow or fast?"

"I don't care. Just get it over with," Patrick said with defeat.

"One more question, Patrick. When I call the cops tonight, and they come over and see you laying on the floor in a pile of blood, who will be the antagonist and who the protagonist?" he asked, opening the envelope.

Dr. Benson pulled the papers out and began rifling through them frantically.

"What the fuck!? What the fuck is this shit!?" he yelled.

Dr. Benson held up one of the papers that read: *You think you're smarter than me?* He looked back at Patrick, who had the same smile on his face as he did when the group of doctors was talking to him at the hospital. The grin got wider as he pulled his hands out from behind the chair.

"Plain old saline is not as powerful as Etorphine, Dr. Benson. I thought you'd have known that."

"What?"

"I knew you would have something ready for me. All I had to do was look in a reasonable spot to find it. And I did."

Dr. Benson slowly took steps back until he hit his chair with the back of his legs. Dumbfounded, he fell into it with a blank look of deflation.

"Why did you let me…?"

"To play with you, Dr. Benson. You are the mouse, and I am the lion. I will bat you around until I see fit to kill you," Patrick said, standing up and walking toward him.

"And now, for the real Etorphine," Patrick said, pulling out the syringe.

Patrick lunged forward quickly, sticking Dr. Benson in the neck. Dr. Benson's head went loose and fell to his shoulder, "Sleep well, Dr. Benson, you'll be needing all the energy you can muster."

★★★★★★★★★★

A long, steady line of drool was flowing from Dr. Benson's mouth and onto his still-clean pajama top. He moaned loudly, swinging his head from side to side, not unlike some of the patients he'd treated. His glasses lay on a table just out of his reach and his thin, brown hair, with its usual part, was laying on his face in random streaks.

"Oh Fab! I'm happy to…to get clean!" Dr. Benson sang, slurring his words and messing up the lyrics.

"Oh Fab, the real borax…in you!"

"Dr. Benson, wake up. It's time for your treatment," Patrick said with a sing-song tone.

"Wha?"

"Yes, that's right. All this I've put you through is coming to a close, finally. You can rest assured the end is almost here."

Dr. Benson thrashed wildly, but he was wasting his energy. He was tied up in a bunker, hands, and feet in shackles that were chained to the wall.

"Take your time, Dr. Benson. I want you one hundred percent aware of what is about to happen," Patrick said with a smile.

TWENTY-SEVEN

"The sixth commandment - 'Thou Shalt Not Kill' fascinated me . . . I always knew that someday I should defy it."

-John Reginald Christie; 8 victims; Calderdale, West Yorkshire England

"ew Hope Police Department, how may I help you?" the desk man answered.

"Yes, this is Gladys Johnston over at New Hope Psychiatric Hospital. I have a bit of a problem. I need to talk to whoever is in charge there. It's an emergency."

"Okay, Ma'am. Well, why don't you describe to me what is happening?"

"We don't have time for this shit. Do you know who Arthur Fritz is?"

"Of course, I know who Arthur Fritz is, lady."

"Well, he's missing from our facility. So is Dr. Benson."

"Oh shit!"

"Yeah, 'Oh, shit.' Now put me through."

Gladys twiddled the phone cord with her thin fingers while the line went silent for a few seconds. If you looked hard enough, you could see a slight tremble in them. Her fingers weren't showing how scared she really was.

"Detective Reynolds."

"Detective, this is Gladys from over at New Hope Hospital. I work for Dr. Benson."

Detective Reynolds was keyed in on the panic in her voice and squinted his eyes in an attempt to focus harder.

"It's Arthur Fritz, he's gone missing. And I have reason to believe that Dr. Benson has been taken by him."

"Okay. Is anyone hurt?"

"No, not yet. I put the place on lockdown, and we have guards searching everywhere now."

"Okay, good. Hold tight. I'm headed that way."

"Thank you, detective. I keep looking over my shoulders like he's going to appear suddenly."

"Try to relax, Gladys."

Gladys just sniffled and put the phone back in its cradle.

★★★★★★★★★★

"Goddammit, Reynolds," Chief Nelson said in disgust.

"I know, Chief. We have men combing the area now."

"This is a fuckin' disaster. I'm gonna have to call the mayor. This ain't gonna be good. I want all the staff interviewed. Start with Gladys."

"Yes, Sir," Detective Reynolds answered.

Chief Nelson took off his cowboy hat and slicked his hair back with his hands, letting out a long sigh.

★★★★★★★★★★

Glady's wide hips were pressing up against the wall as she could only bite her fingernails to release her anxiety. Another orderly had let Detective Reynolds in the building and up the stairs to the hallway where Gladys and some of the other staff members were checking on the locked-up patients.

"Gladys, I'm Detective Reynolds."

"Pleasure Detective."

"I know you're upset, but try to do the best you can. Tell me about Arthur going missing?"

"He was in his cell last night for headcount. I'm usually one of the first ones here in the morning. David, one of the orderlies, said he didn't come out for breakfast. They went into his cell, and he was gone. I put the place on lockdown. All the patients had to get back to their cells."

"Now, Gladys, you said you have reason to believe Dr. Benson was taken by Arthur? What makes you think that?" Detective Reynolds asked from Dr. Benson's chair.

"The doctor, he's...he's been actin' real strange lately, Detective. Kinda like he's on edge."

Gladys' southern accent got thick as the fear took hold of her.

"Like how?"

"Showin' up with cuts on his face, bags under his eyes. Somethin' wasn't right. I could just tell. I knew too, I had a weird feeling Arthur was up to something. He just gave me the willies every time he was near me."

"When was the last time you saw Dr. Benson?"

"Yesterday. I told him to go home. He looked like he hadn't slept in a week. He went on home, and when we found out Arthur was missing, I called his house, and there was no answer. I was a little worried, so I drove over to his house. The front door was open, and his car was gone. That's when I really knew something was amiss, and I called you."

"Okay. You're doing good, Gladys. We are going to find Dr. Benson, all right?"

"You know what Arthur is capable of, Detective. Poor Dr. Benson," Gladys said, breaking down in tears.

"Here now, try to relax, okay?" Detective Reynolds said, handing her his handkerchief.

After Detective Reynolds had spoken with some other staff members, he met back up with Chief Nelson, just outside of the hospital. The sun was starting to go down, and they both needed a smoke break after a long day.

"Who in the hell thought that red light was a good idea?" Chief barked, lighting up a smoke.

"It's pretty creepy, Sir. So, we have the staff interviewed. Nobody seems to know anything. Most of them say that Arthur was calm and quiet. Hung around another feller named George. But for the most part, they say he was a nice guy."

"Yeah, nice until he carves you up. Or rips your damn heart out. That's what we're dealing with here, Reynolds, a goddamn animal," Chief Nelson said, shaking his head.

"I'm going to call the guys off for now. We need to get back to the station and regroup."

"Good idea, Reynolds. I'm going to head back and get my ass chewed out by the Mayor. Have them boys get some rest. This ain't over until we catch the bastard again, you hear?"

"Yes, Sir."

★★★★★★★★★★

Chief Nelson waddled down the hallway, exhausted from a long day of work and from anticipating the conversation with Mayor Jenkins.

"Come on in," Jenkins yelled.

Chief Nelson removed his hat, breathing heavily and still trying to catch his breath from the walk down the long hall. Mayor Jenkins was pacing the floor in his office with a drink in his hand.

"You'd better have some good news for me, Chief," he barked.

"Nothing yet, Don. We are pulling the boys back in to talk about our strategy for getting this guy."

"Fuck, Nelson! Am I going to have to call in the feds? Am I going to have to wake my friends up and tell them that I can't handle my shit over here in the lovely town of New Hope?! There is more here at stake than you'll ever know, Nelson," Jenkins yelled in frustration.

Chief Nelson remained calm and serious under the pressure, "Give us one more day. We still have some places to look. Then you might want to consider bringing in some help."

"Well, what are your thoughts? Do you think he's left town? Is Benson alive?"

"I don't know that, Don."

"The press is going to have my ass tomorrow morning. Word is already starting to get out. It's a damn mess. The sad part is we were just in this situation, Nelson."

"I know. And we'll get back out of it."

All the fears that Don Jenkins had when Dr. Benson first told him about someone knowing their little secret was starting to come true. The whole while he was talking about Arthur with Chief Nelson, Jenkins was actually wondering if Arthur was the one who knew and how safe he really was.

"Let me tell you something, Chief. You tell your boys in a roundabout way, but you find this son of a bitch, and you kill him. You hear me? I don't want this town dragged through another court case. They want justice."

"It was always my intention."

"My secretary has the details on a press conference in the morning. I want you there. Now get out of my office. I'm sure you have things to do."

"Yes, Sir."

The proverbial shit was rolling downhill and right on top of Chief Nelson. It would only be a matter of hours before the town was in full panic mode once again. And to top it off, those in the search had zero clues where Patrick and Dr. Benson could be.

★★★★★★★★★★

Dr. Benson yelled as loudly as he could, but he only got back echoes from the cold, cement walls. The Etorphine had done quite a number on him, taking him nearly the whole day to come to. He wiggled his bare feet to warm them. They had become quite cold from lying on the concrete floor. The room was slightly blurred without his glasses, and he couldn't make out any details in the dim light.

"Help!" he continued to scream.

With his voice starting to go hoarse and his energy waning, the sound of the lock opening perked him up quickly.

"Who's there!?"

The squeaky doorknob on the metal door pierced through the silent room that was now filled by a squinted eyed Dr. Benson.

"You're awake. I'm so glad to see that."

"Patrick?"

"No, Harold. Patrick isn't here right now. But he told me to bring you some food."

"Arthur! Thank god!" Dr. Benson could only see a dark and faceless shadow. "Arthur, please get me my glasses."

Arthur obliged and gently put them on his face, bringing him clearly into view.

"Arthur, please. You have to let me out of here. Patrick is going to kill me," Dr. Benson pleaded.

"Harold, now you know I can't do that. I don't want to be on his bad side like you."

"What did I do to get there?"

"He told me, Harold. Not good," Arthur said, shaking his head.

"You know they're out looking for us, right? I bet the whole town is out there."

"I would say that whole town is not out looking. I would say the whole town is shaking right now because Patrick, I mean me, is on the loose. Finding you is second on their list. Here, you need to eat."

"Where are we?"

"Another bunker Patrick built, just like the first," Arthur said, handing him a tray of food.

"Arthur, listen to me, man. Can you let me out?"

"No, Harold. I'm afraid this is what you wanted."

"Look! I can help you. I know why you're like this. It was Mr. Dale. He hurt you, Arthur! But it's not your fault. Let me help you!"

"I can't choose between you and Patrick."

"Is he here? Let me talk to him," Dr. Benson pleaded.

"He's here."

Arthur's facial expressions went from a calm and loose demeanor to a gritty and teeth-clenched snarl.

"Dr. Benson, are you trying to talk your way out of here? Did you think I would just leave you to the care of Arthur?"

"You're fuckin' crazy Patrick. They're going to get you, and they will kill you."

"Shhh, Dr. Benson. Don't get all worked up. You are going to die, and that's that. How you die, is a different story."

Dr. Benson began sobbing, and soon his glasses fogged up from the tears.

"Why are you doing this?" Dr. Benson cried.

Patrick stood up, towering over the restrained Dr. Benson.

"There it is! Right on cue, Dr. Benson! Let's hear the begging and the pleading!" Patrick said, clapping and laughing his twisted and sick laugh.

"I think you know why I'm doing this."

Snot dripped and ran from Dr. Benson's nose. The whole time he wondered if this was God punishing him for his sins. But he quickly came to the realization that this was who Patrick was. Crazy. No disease classification, no behavior issues, and no excuse, just good, old- fashioned, bat-shit crazy.

"Patrick?"

"Yes, Dr. Benson?"

"Will you make it quick?"

"My, you went through the stages of death terribly quickly, Dr. Benson, but I'll answer your question with another question. Have I ever made it quick?"

Dr. Benson dropped his head in despair. Patrick had been planning this from the get-go. Making a set of keys, building a second bunker, hiding the phony pictures in his shed and even putting saline in a syringe to trick him into thinking he had him dead to rights. Yes, he was on the tail end of the long game, and it would not be long before he lost.

Patrick moved over to Dr. Benson's left side and unlocked one of the locks, freeing his hand from the shackle. He stood back up and kicked the plate that held what looked like a ham and cheese sandwich.

"Eat. We have lots of things to do before it's over. Are you afraid of the dark? I hope you are," Patrick said, clicking off the light and slamming the door.

Not a sliver of light could be seen, not even from the cracks around the door. Patrick's footsteps could be heard going up the stairs. Dr. Benson tried to listen, but being underground dampened the sound quite a bit. Then he heard it, the faint sound of a motor starting.

"Come on, man. You are smart. You can get out of this," he said aloud while taking a bite of the sandwich. "Ugh, what the hell is this?"

The bread was crusty and stale and whatever meat it was seemed to be tough and chewy. It didn't matter. He was hungry enough to eat anything. As he sat there chewing his food, he realized there was no way out. He was shackled in padlocks, and he had nothing. He was going to have to use his mouth and his brain to talk his way out of this one.

"Think!" he said with a mouth full of food.

TWENTY-EIGHT

"Take your worst nightmares, and put my face to them."

-Tommy Lynn Sells; 22 victims; Holcomb, Missouri USA

M ayor Jenkins paced the tiled bricks that lined his fenced in back patio. He was going on his fourth Pall Mall cigarette, chain-smoking from all the stress. There was much more at stake here than just catching Arthur Fritz. Reputations were on the line and not just his. Who knew who else was exposed? He crushed his smoke out on the ground with his foot and walked back in the house. It was time to make a phone call.

"Albert. Don Jenkins here."

"Don? It's late. What's going on?" the voice said on the other end of the line.

"Yes, I know. I'm, well, I'm in a pickle here, Albert."

Albert cleared his throat and spoke as if he had suddenly woken up, "What's going on?"

"Well, for one, I have Arthur Fritz on the loose," Jenkins said.

"Good Lord, Don. What the hell happened?"

"That's not all, Albert. He probably knows about what we do. I think he even has evidence."

Jenkins loosened his tie in an attempt to gain more air, "Don, this isn't good. You could get a lot of people in trouble with this."

"I know that, Albert. That's why I'm calling. I need some help. I need some reinforcements. I need him caught and dead. We need him caught and dead."

"I'll send an agent out first thing tomorrow."

"Thank you, Albert."

"Don?"

"Yes, Albert?"

"I don't have to tell you what kind of shit you are in if this escalates any higher, do I? They'll have you and me both killed. This club operates entirely underground. People have disappeared for merely threatening to tell someone else or the news."

"I'm aware of that, Albert. Now just send someone. Your best guy."

"He'll be there tomorrow."

Jenkins hung up the phone and grabbed his cigarettes off the counter to head back for another smoke. Turning around to face the back door, he suddenly found himself face to face with Patrick.

"Arthur?" Jenkins said, befuddled.

Those were the only words he could get out before the pipe came across his vision and hit him in the head. Jenkins fell to the floor with a loud plop, but not before crashing into a table by the doorway and spilling pictures and a flower vase on the floor.

"Don?" a woman's voice from upstairs called out. "Don! What happened?"

Viola came down the stairs and into the kitchen, flicking on the big light to see what was going on. There was nothing but broken glass and an end table scattered on the floor. A cold breeze drifted in through the open back door and went clean through her nightgown, adding to the goosebumps she already had from being on edge. She ran to the phone and started moving the rotary dials.

"Nelson!"

"Who is this?"

"It's Viola. Something happened. I think Don has been taken."

"Oh, shit! I'll be right over."

"Hurry, I'm all alone."

★★★★★★★★★★

Dr. Benson was somewhat sleeping but, the crick in his neck didn't allow him to get fully comfortable. In the total silence, he heard a car pulling up, perking him up.

"Help!" he yelled, as the lock on the door popped open.

The metal door swung open, letting in some of the moonlight. And with the pull of a string, the light came on, slightly blinding Dr. Benson.

"Help!" Dr. Benson screamed louder.

"Yell all you want, Dr. Benson. We are so far removed that no one will ever hear you," Patrick said, hauling the unconscious Don Jenkins in. Patrick let out a grunt just after dropping Don on the concrete near the wall opposite Dr. Benson. Patrick propped Don up against the wall and started buckling his arms over his head and locking them in.

"Patrick. Oh, fuck! What are you doing?" Dr. Benson uttered.

"Oh, Dr. Benson, we are in for a treat today. It's time to learn."

"Learn what?"

Patrick ignored his last question and continued locking the shackles. Blood from where the pipe struck him trickled down the side of Don's temple and onto his button-up shirt.

"What did you do to him?"

"Relax, Dr. Benson. I just knocked him out," Patrick replied, giving Don a little slap on the cheeks.

"I see you enjoyed your dinner," Patrick said as he leaned down, picked up the plate, and set it on the table near the door.

"You're in deep shit, Patrick. It's not too late. Let us go. We can go back to the way things were."

"The way things were?" Patrick snarled. "You think this was all some path that was forced upon me, and that I'm on the run now? Wake up, Dr. Benson! This was all planned. This was laid out months before I even got myself caught."

"You got yourself caught?"

"Of course. What started out as a hobby became an obsession. Killing is fun, but it's better when the target can fight back. I would say you being a doctor and me being locked in a cell is fair."

"You're fuckin' sick."

"You keep saying that. By calling me 'sick' over and over, do you expect me to be Mr. Humanitarian suddenly? Mr. Nice Guy? I'm crazy! I'm a crazy, Dr. Benson!"

While Patrick and Dr. Benson talked, Don Jenkins finally started to stir.

"Ugh," he moaned.

"Ah, Mr. Jenkins. Welcome to the party," Patrick said in a delighted tone.

Jenkins looked up to see Dr. Benson sitting right across from him. Patrick just watched the two interact from the sideline.

"Harold. What the fuck?" Jenkins said, shaking his head in dismay.

Patrick just laughed like a child watching two animals turn on each other. "Yes, Harold, what the fuck?" Patrick mocked.

"What do you want with us?" Jenkins asked.

"In short, I want to kill you."

"Look, man. I'm connected. All the way to D.C. Bigwigs. I can get all of this cleared up and swept away," Jenkins mumbled.

"Look at him, Dr. Benson. Trading away anything in the name of self-preservation. Remember when you were like that?" Patrick said, smiling happily.

Patrick stood up from leaning on the table and put his hands together as if getting prepared to work, "Okay, fellas. Dr. Benson here is growing. And to grow you need to experience pain. We've tried this before, and it didn't take. But something tells me this time it will."

Dr. Benson knew exactly what he was talking about. He was talking about Mrs. Buselli.

"So, Dr. Benson, I will now be handing over total control to you," Patrick said, reaching into his pocket.

He pulled out the snub nose revolver that belonged or used to belong, to Dr. Benson.

"There is one bullet in here, all lined up and ready to fire," he said, palming the gun.

"You know what you have to do, Dr. Benson. You need to kill Mr. Jenkins here. Now, remember. When I hand you the gun, your natural response is going to be to shoot me. I warn you, though. Go right ahead if you like, but I assure you that nobody will find you here and you will die the most agonizing death imaginable. As you can see over there, I have plenty of water for you. This will get you about three weeks of life. But without food, your body will wither away and begin to eat itself. I even hear that the mind will start to fade in and out. It's quite terrifying."

Patrick turned the gun and grabbed it by the barrel, extending it out safely to Dr. Benson, whose left hand was still free from when he was given dinner.

"So, shoot me if you must. I completely understand if you have to. Just remember the fate you will be sealing for you and your friend here," Patrick said, handing him the gun.

Dr. Benson looked over at Don before slowly grabbing the gun. Once in his hand, he immediately turned it on, Patrick.

"Ah! There is that instinct! Do it, Dr. Benson! Shoot me! Come on! You are in control now! Isn't that what you wanted? Here is that power you love so much. I've given it to you as a gift. Now use it, you goddamn coward. Shoot me!" Patrick yelled.

The gun trembled like a leaf in the wind. Dr. Benson began to sweat before lowering the gun and dropping his head.

"Now, do the right thing and shoot Mr. Jenkins."

"Harold, you can't do that, man. How long have I known you?"

"It was wrong, Don, those boys, it was all wrong. We are the sick ones. We shouldn't have done that to them," Dr. Benson said in a cracked voice.

Patrick only smiled glibly.

"Harold, you can't kill me! Think about this," Jenkins pleaded.

"Patrick? What will happen to me if I do this?" Dr. Benson asked in defeat.

"We can reevaluate your progress and see if further treatment is needed."

"Harold! No!" Jenkins pleaded.

Dr. Benson raised the gun up and pointed it at Jenkins while Patrick stood back with his fingers in his ears. Patrick made it sound as if there was a chance that Dr. Benson would come out of this unscathed.

"This is what we deserve for that. Tommy Buselli, Jacob Peters, all of them, Don. Did you really think we wouldn't get punished for it?"

"He's not the one who judges us, Harold. Arthur, look, you can take us to court. We will confess to everything. Please," Jenkins said sobbing.

"This is a court, Mr. Jenkins. You have been tried and found guilty. Now, do it, Dr. Benson, before my patience wears thin, and I change my mind about not hurting you," Patrick rebutted.

The gun still shook in the air as it reached out in front of Dr. Benson. Both men cried as neither wanted to be in their respective situations but seemed powerless to stop it.

"Right in the chest. He'll bleed out. Or, in the head, if you are a compassionate person. And if you miss, I have more bullets. Or, you can use it on yourself. There's always that option, Dr. Benson."

Jenkins squirmed, but it was of no use. He gaped down fate in the form of the little black gun that waved across from him. Dr. Benson looked his best friend in the eye. He lowered the gun and his head, only to pick them both back up and pull the trigger.

Bang! The ringing from the gunshot in the tiny, confined space was deafening. Dr. Benson started crying and tossed the gun onto the ground.

"Bravo, Dr. Benson. But you shot him in the stomach! It's a shame for Mr. Jenkins. That could take a few days," Patrick said laughing.

Jenkins moaned in pain as a red spot began to form on his still neatly pressed white shirt.

"Ugh! Harold!" Jenkins yelled out in pain.

"I'm sorry, Don. I'm so fuckin' sorry."

"Don't be sorry, Dr. Benson. You did it. It wasn't that hard, was it? I mean he's not dead yet, but sooner or later an infection will get him. A gut shot is harrowing. Right, Mr. Jenkins?"

Dr. Benson didn't say anything. He just sat there, realizing what he had just done.

"Well, I'm off to bed. I'm quite tired. I'll leave you two here to sort things out. Lights on or off?" Patrick asked. "I'll leave them on this time."

TWENTY-NINE

"It was the power and domination and seeing the fear. That was more exciting than actually causing the harm."

-John Joubert; 3 victims; Lawrence, Massachusetts USA

November 16, 1967

It's been a long and hard fall for me. I've been working diligently to get all the pieces in play for the big chess match. I work all day on projects and things I'll need, and at night I study from psychology books. I wouldn't say I'm nervous to get caught--more excited than nervous, I guess. Everything seems to be in place. I've gone over the plan many times, on paper and in my head. Now it's time to turn myself in and confess to everything. If they give me the chair, they give me the chair, but I have a feeling I can act crazy enough to end up in the fancy new hospital.

I'm anxious to meet Dr. Benson. I've admired him from afar, and soon, I hope to be face to face with him. I want to learn what scares him. I want to know what excites him...I want to kill him. Tomorrow my plan is to follow Detective Reynolds around until he goes into a public place. After that,

I plan to walk in with blood all over me and confess to the murders that have had this town in a panic. It'll ease their precious little minds, but only for a bit. After what I have planned, the fear level should go up tenfold. It's one thing to be afraid of what you don't know; it's another to know what something is and know there is nothing you can do about it. New Hope will be my playground.

This will be my last entry for a while. It's time to get to work and earn the big payoff. I've thought a lot about what I will do after this. I certainly won't be welcomed here. Arthur has talked about moving out West. He would like to visit the ocean. As for me...I have a natural tendency to hate hippies. They are leeches on society, and California would be ripe with them. I can see myself walking the beach and looking at all the beautiful people. Yeah...maybe that's what we'll do.

—Patrick

THIRTY

"Killing prostitutes had become an obsession with me. I could not stop myself. It was like a drug."

-Peter Sutcliffe; 13 victims; Bingley England

hief Nelson's phone had been ringing off the hook all day. TV stations and newspapers were calling from all over the country. The tiny town of New Hope was back on the map, and not for a good reason. The town and surrounding area were in an uproar about Arthur Fritz being on the loose. Now a doctor and the mayor were missing as well. Viola Jenkins was so frantic that one of the doctors from New Hope Psychiatrist Hospital had to sedate her.

"Dammit, Martha! Tell them we have a press conference in one hour, in front of the courthouse. Shit! I can hardly think with that damn phone ringing like that!"

Nelson was taking out his frustration on his secretary, Martha. But he had no clue as to the whereabouts of any of them. For all he knew, Arthur had taken them across the country and killed them in the middle of nowhere. The fear of never finding them came across strong.

"Chief?" Martha said, knocking on the door.

"Yeah?"

"I have an Agent Adams here looking for you."

"Send 'em on in."

Chief Nelson sat up from his desk, his big belly barely squeezing between the desk and his chair. Martha opened the door and in walked a clean shaven, young man wearing a jacket, tie, and a hat.

"I'm Chief Nelson. How can I help you?" he asked, extending his hand.

The young man took his hat off and shook the chief's hand. "I'm Special Agent Adams from the Federal Bureau of Investigation. I was sent here by Senator Albert Young."

"Please," Chief Nelson said, opening his palm in the direction of the chair.

Chief Nelson was relieved to have help on the case, but he would never know how close he was to not actually getting it.

"I'll be pretty blunt, Chief. I'm here to fix your shit and the mess your town is in. I will be taking charge of all your people and this investigation. It must be bad because they don't send me on the easy ones. Is there any problem with that?"

"No, Sir."

"Good, now fill me in on exactly what is going on."

As Chief Nelson gave Agent Adams all the details he needed to get started, Agent Adams took vigorous notes, asking questions about every little detail.

"Who was the arresting officer or detective for Arthur Fritz?"

"That would be Detective Reynolds. He's out in the field searching for them."

"Get all your men back here, Chief. Now."

"But they need…"

"I said now. Get them in here," Agent Adams said, raising his voice.

"Right away."

Chief Nelson picked up the radio that connected to dispatch and gave the order for all the men to come back to the station.

"Do you have a press conference scheduled?" Agent Adams asked.

"Yes. In one hour."

"Good. At least you've done one thing right," he said sarcastically.

A few minutes had passed with Agent Adams learning all he could about the most recent events. Before long, Detective Reynolds and a few other officers started coming into the station.

"Gather up, men," Chief Nelson barked to the crowd.

Chief Nelson and Agent Adams walked out of the office and into the main office space. Detective Reynolds and the others huddle around.

"Everyone, this is Special Agent Adams. He's with the Bureau. He's taking control of this investigation, so listen up."

"Thank you, Chief. As he said, I am Special Agent Adams. You will take your orders directly from me. Is that understood?"

No one in the room liked a stranger coming in and telling everyone what to do, but the situation seemed so dire that everyone reluctantly accepted Agent Adams's leadership.

"I can only assume you're Detective Reynolds because you're not in a uniform?"

"That's correct," Detective Reynolds replied.

"Tell me briefly, how did you apprehend Arthur Fritz?" Adams said with his pen in hand, ready to write.

"What does that have to do with the mayor and Benson?" Reynolds replied.

"Don't you fuckin' worry about that detective. You guys already mucked this up the first time. I'll be damned if they send me to your shitty little town to clean this up and I let you do it again."

Detective Reynolds didn't remember a time when he was talked to like that, but he submitted and answered the question.

"I was eating lunch at Pearl's Diner on Main. He came in, and the whole room went quiet.

He had blood all over his clothes, started ranting about killing people and that he was the murderer and someone else was making him do it. It was just a bunch of rambling. I dropped my food, and I went over and slowly put him in cuffs. I brought him back here, and he confessed to everything and showed us where all the bodies were. It was horrible."

"So, he just walked in and surrendered?"

"Yup. Kept on about how someone else was making him do these awful things."

"Thank you, Detective."

Reynolds just gave a slight head nod while Agent Adams turned around with his back to the officers.

"Okay. If he willingly gave himself up, that means he might have had this planned. Detective, right after this press conference, I want you to take me to the hospital so I can speak with the staff. The rest of you will be organizing a search with volunteers. This town isn't that big. He's here somewhere. When we find Fritz, we'll find the other two."

Agent Adams's hothead didn't exactly put the police force at ease, but they wouldn't say no to the leadership he provided. It finally felt like there was a plan to find the missing individuals. As reporters gathered outside city hall, Chief Nelson and Agent Adams prepared to talk. The podium was set up with a few microphones crudely taped to it. A camera crew had even come up from Washington D.C. to cover the story. People in the crowd were grumbling and angry, not unlike the town hall meeting before.

"Thank you all for coming out. I have an update for you all and will share some news," Chief Nelson began, while Agent Adams stood by, patiently waiting for his turn to go up. "As of right now, there aren't any traces of Mayor Jenkins or Dr. Benson. All our searches have turned up empty. But, we are lucky to have some new help. Let me introduce Special Agent Adams from the FBI." Chief bowed out of the way, and Agent Adams stepped up. Before Adams could speak, a man from the crowd yelled out.

"What are you going to do to help us? We're scared shitless over here!"

"I know you are. I can see that you are shook up as a town. You're scared for yourself and for your families, I get that. I also see a lot of energy here, so I'm asking for volunteers. If you want to help, we need to form a search party. If you have firearms, you can bring them, but we need to be safe. If you want to do something, this is how you can help. We need to scour this place, and all the surrounding areas, too."

Head nods and fists being clenched could be seen in the crowd.

"If you want to volunteer, form up over here right after this. Officer Lamar will be leading the search."

Very quickly, Agent Adams had turned the small search party of four or five into fifty or sixty. More questions came from the reporters and the people, but Agent Adams handled them all calmly and decisively.

After the press conference was over, Agent Adams pulled Officer Lamar over to the side, "Listen, Officer. You guys be careful out there. I want you looking in any abandoned houses you have. I want all the area down by the river searched."

"Yes, Sir."

"And, one more thing. You tell these men that if they see Arthur Fritz, they are to shoot first and we will answer questions later. You hear me?"

"Yes, Sir."

"Good. Now, go lead these people."

★★★★★★★★★★

Agent Adams stepped out from the squad car that Detective Reynolds had parked right in front of New Hope Psychiatric Hospital. He looked up at the building and shielded his eyes from the sun.

"So, this is it huh? The hospital that Dr. Benson created for the criminally insane?"

"Yup. It is quite a big deal for our town, Sir," Reynolds replied.

"Well, let's get in there. I need to ask some questions."

"This way," Reynolds said, pointing to the main entrance.

"Gladys, this is Special Agent Adams. He'd like to ask you a few questions," Detective Reynolds said as he introduced the two.

"Nice to meet you," she said, shaking his hand.

"You as well. Now, Gladys, did Arthur have any reason to dislike Dr. Benson? Did there seem to be any hatred?"

"No, Arthur was a calm guy. He gave me the creeps, but he was never mean. He was very kind to the staff and everyone else. Dr. Benson did mention another personality that Arthur had. I think Dr. Benson said his name was Patrick."

Agent Adams diligently took notes while continuing to listen and think of his next question. Like a hound dog, he was sniffing out clues.

"And Arthur was accounted for on the nightly lockdown?"

"Yes, Sir. Our staff goes through and gets a visual on every patient when they are in their cells for nightly lockdown. I spoke with the staff member, and he remembers seeing Arthur sitting at his desk, writing that night."

"Hmmm. Any idea how he got out?"

"Not one clue, Agent Adams. We are all wondering that same thing."

"May I see his cell?" Agent Adams asked.

"Certainly. Follow me."

The trio left the small meeting room downstairs and went into the general population area. The hospital was still on lockdown on orders from Dr. Holcombe, who was acting Chief of the hospital.

"Here it is," Gladys said, pointing toward the closed door.

Adams kneeled on the tile and carefully inspected the exterior hinges. Then he moved his fingers around the edge of the door, looking for anything out of the ordinary.

"Would you like me to unlock the door?"

"Yes, please."

Adams walked into the room slowly, holding his breath as if not to disturb the scene. The bed was neatly made, and the plastic chair was tucked in neatly under the desk.

"Did anybody touch this area after he was found to be missing?"

"No," Gladys replied.

"And was the door open or shut?"

"It was closed and locked."

Agent Adams moved back over to the door and inspected the interior part of the door jamb. He couldn't find any indications that the door was tampered with and quickly moved on.

"Okay. Thank you very much. Gladys, do you mind if I speak with Detective Reynolds alone for a minute?"

"Not at all. Let me walk you down to the conference room so you can have some privacy."

Gladys closed the conference room door behind her, leaving only Detective Reynolds and Agent Adams in the small, one-table room.

"One thing is clear, Detective. Arthur had help getting out of here, but how? How is this all connected?" Agent Adams said, thinking out loud.

Detective Reynolds was in awe of Agent Adams's intuition and knack for following a trail of invisible breadcrumbs. He could easily see why he was brought in.

"You interviewed the rest of the staff, is that correct?"

"Yes, that's correct," Reynolds replied.

"And did anything seem fishy about them?"

"No. I mean they are all good workers. Black guys mostly. They are happy to have such a well-paying job."

"And the key inventory. Were any missing or unaccounted for?"

"No. They were all there."

Agent Adams paced around the room, reviewing his notes.

"Where are you going with this, Agent Adams?"

"Can't you see it? Someone helped him out of here. That's the only explanation. Those locks are unpickable. Top-of-the-line, prison-grade locks. And you saw that door. The only way through it was with a cutting torch or a key. And I didn't see any burn marks, did you?"

"No. So that only leaves one thing. He had a key made."

"Yes! Hey, all these government facilities are required to have all their building information on hand. Somewhere in here are all the records for the contracts. That means whoever installed the doors and locks should be on file. Let's go get Gladys and find out who."

THIRTY-ONE

"That is my ambition, to have killed more people. More helpless people than any man or woman who has ever lived."

-Jane Toppan; 33 victims; Boston, Massachusetts USA

Gladys led the way down the dark basement hallway, Detective Reynolds and Agent Adams in tow. Gladys' hips swung back and forth before stopping at the boiler room door.

"This is our boiler room. Maintenance said this is where all the records are," she said, turning the key.

A couple of men were down there working on some pipes and chatting when they walked in.

"Hey, fellas. Don't worry about us. We just need to find some of the contracts for this building," Gladys said.

The older of the two men pointed toward the corner to the tall, green filing cabinet with his wrench. Agent Adams and Detective Reynolds scurried over and began opening drawers, rifling through a mess of paperwork. After nearly an hour of shuffling through all the papers, they came up empty.

"Fuck. It's like the very one we need is missing," Agent Adams said out loud.

"Hey, check behind the file cabinet. A bunch of shit seems to pile up back there," the maintenance man said very sarcastically as if he knew who it was.

Detective Reynolds squatted down and looked behind the cabinet. Sure enough, covered in dust, there were a few pieces of paper stapled together. He blew off the dust and handed it to Agent Adams. Agent Adams walked over to the middle of the room, directly under the light to get a better view. He flipped through pages until he found the key contract. There in bold letters was his answer as to who helped Arthur get out.

Cell and Lock Contract

Lead Contract: Vermont Lock and Key
Lead contractor: James Fenton
Installer: Patrick Leopold

Agent Adams rolled up the papers and slapped them repeatedly against his leg.

"I was right. He had help."

"From who?" Gladys asked.

"Himself, assuming he gave himself the last name of Leopold," Agent Adams said, pointing to the name on the paper.

A pale white glow came over Gladys. Her instinct about Arthur had been spot on. Knowing that he had access to go in and out as he pleased sent chills down her back.

"Gladys, thank you for your help. I'm going to keep these, I'll bring them back."

"You're welcome."

"Let's go, Reynolds."

****

"Listen, Reynolds, Dr. Benson and the mayor are in deep shit," Agent Adams said in the car.

"Why is that?"

"Don't you see? Arthur gave himself up. He was in on all this shit for a long time. He's been hunting Dr. Benson. And now he has him."

"Fuck!" Reynolds said, hitting the steering wheel.

"'Fuck' is right. And if he had this planned out for a while, then only God knows where they are now. Let's go out to his house. I want to look around there."

"Yes, Sir."

Detective Reynolds pulled the car to an abrupt stop in front of Arthur Fritz' house.

"When was the last time anyone's been out here?"

"I came out here yesterday during the search."

"Did you check out the house?" Agent Adams asked.

"I went in yesterday. I tried to get into the bunker over there, but my key didn't work."

"Your key didn't work? And you didn't find that strange?"

"Not really. Figured one of the other guys changed it or something."

"Goddamn it, Reynolds. You have completely fucked this case up, you know that?"

Detective Reynolds hung his head down. Agent Adams was right. They really hadn't done anything right. Even Arthur turned himself in.

"Don't get down on yourself. But this is basic detective shit. And I'm probably guessing you guys don't get a lot of action down here like this," Adams said in an apologetic tone.

Detective Reynolds followed Agent Adams around the house for a quick visual inspection and then over to the bunker, which looked like a roof resting on the ground.

"God this fucker was sick. Did I read right that he was killing people in here? Built it specifically for that?"

"That's right. That's what he said."

"What a crazy son of a bitch," Adams said, shaking his head.

Agent Adams walked down the concrete steps and paused just before the door, sniffing the air.

"Phew!" Agent Adams yelled out.

"Can you smell that?"

"Yeah. Smells like a rotting carcass," Reynolds replied.

They both looked at each other with surprised looks.

"Stand back," Agent Adams said, taking a step back up the stairs.

He drew out his .357 Magnum and pointed it at the lock, turning his head in the process. He squeezed the trigger, and the hammer came back until a loud bang reverberated out.

"Fuck! That's loud!" Adams yelled out.

The lock dropped to the floor and bounced off the concrete. Adams opened the door slowly, while Reynolds peeked down the stairwell to see what was down there. The smell hit Adams like a bus.

"Goddamn it, mother fucker!" he yelled.

"Good Lord," Reynolds said, making the sign of the cross when he saw the silhouette of a body in the corner.

Adams pulled his shirt over his mouth and nose with his right hand while pulling a flashlight out of his jacket with his left. Reynolds followed suit and crept in the bunker slowly, with his shirt over his mouth.

"We got a body here. Female. Slashed throat. Call it in, Reynolds!" Adams said.

"Oh, God. Lots of decomp here. Maggots are already eating the body up," Reynolds said, swatting flies away with his free hand.

The dried blood on the floor and the walls faded to a dark maroon and was no longer the bright red it once was. Adams looked around in amazement and barely started to get a feel for the kind of crazy he was dealing with. Back at the car, Reynolds called Chief Nelson to get some back up out there, while Adams kicked the dirt around, looking for an explanation for why a human being would do the things he had heard about and just saw. No answers were found.

"Reynolds. You got any theories as to where this guy is? Come on. You've been quiet. I know you're thinking in that head of yours. What do you have?" Agent Adams asked gently.

"Well, I think he's still here. In this town, somewhere. It's apparent that he wanted Dr. Benson for some reason. And based on all his victim profiles, he likes to torture and inflict pain on them. So, it makes me think that he's still here, and maybe Benson and the mayor are still alive."

"Outstanding, Reynolds. Those were my thoughts, too. Anything else?"

"He's been planning this for a while, right? So, they must be in some remote place. Maybe that he owns or something."

"Yes. I was thinking that, too. He's around here. I just know it," Adams said, looking around the property.

★★★★★★★★★★

"I'm sorry, Don. I'm fuckin' sorry," Dr. Benson said over and over.

"Stop it, Harold. I'm not angry. I get it now. I get how crazy this bastard is. We were fucked from a long time ago," Jenkins said, grunting in pain.

"How are you feeling?" Dr. Benson asked.

"It hurts. It's fuckin' painful. I could use a smoke right now."

"Me, too."

"You think there's a way we get out alive?" Jenkins asked with an optimistic tone.

"Not a snowball's chance in hell, Don. I know this guy. He's been toying with me for weeks now. I realize it was his intention all along. We're going to die here."

"Fuck!" Jenkins yelled out in pain.

"I'm sorry, Don. I'm sorry for everything I've ever done wrong," Dr. Benson said crying.

"Me, too, Harold," Jenkins said with his eyes closed.

Dr. Benson and Mayor Jenkins sat there, trying to sleep, but mostly pondering the series of events which led them to be tied to the walls and floors in the bunker of a mad man. Every single choice they made led here. Dr. Benson could only sob, as he couldn't come up with anyone to blame except himself.

Night crept in, and Dr. Benson reached for a jug of water. His free left hand had to cross his body, and he could barely grab the handle, dragging it over.

"You awake, Don?"

"Ehh…"

Jenkins didn't answer, he just moaned and took the pain. Sweat beads were forming and running down his face. His body temperature was rising, most likely from an infection setting in.

"Hang in there, Don," Dr. Benson said, taking a drink of the water.

He realized what Patrick had told him about the water keeping him alive for three weeks. Looking back on it now, he would have chosen to use that bullet on himself had he not been so doubtful about the capabilities and drive of Patrick.

★★★★★★★★★★

The lock on the outside of the door started to jiggle, and Dr. Benson perked up quickly.

"Don. Psst! Wake up. He's here," Dr. Benson whispered.

Don Jenkins sat immobile and unaware of what was happening. Infection was setting in, soon he would be screaming in pain until the very end.

The door cracked open slowly to reveal Patrick's face. Dr. Benson didn't know if he was disappointed or excited, disappointed that it wasn't help, or excited that it was Patrick to put him out of his misery.

"Hello, there," Patrick said.

Dr. Benson didn't reply.

"I'm sorry I had to leave. I had to get a few things before I skip town. How is our friend?" Patrick said, bending down to get a closer look.

"Oh," he winced, "He doesn't look too good. Oh, well. Let us get on with our last session, shall we, Dr. Benson?"

"Are you going to reevaluate me?"

"No, Dr. Benson. I'm going to kill you."

Patrick looked more calm and relaxed than Dr. Benson ever remembered seeing him. "This moment feels surreal, doesn't it? I mean, so much work on my part to get to this point, and here it is. As they say, it's about the journey and not about the destination. You have taught me patience and forward thinking more than anything. And I thank you for that."

"Skip the shit, Patrick. Just get it over with. I'm exhausted."

"Don't be angry, Dr. Benson. It'll come. But I want to tell you a story first. A fascinating, true story that relates to us a lot. Arthur read me a story one time, I believe it was a National Geographic, fantastic magazine. It was about this tribe in Africa and how they hunt gazelles. As you know, some tribes use traps, others use spears, and the lions, of course, use brute force. Well, the tribe we read about uses endurance. Instead of killing the gazelle or zebra with a tool, they run the animal down, sometimes well over seventy miles. Can you believe that? Seventy miles, Dr. Benson. The animal runs and runs, but the hunter never gives up. It's a battle of will power. Who will give up first? The animal would stop to get a rest and so would the hunters, never getting out of sight of each other. The animal scared, knowing that this creature will stop at nothing to get it. It's almost like a nightmare, where someone is chasing you, and you can never get away.

Finally, the tired animal lays down and accepts its fate. The hunter then walks up to the docile beast, thanks it, and quickly slits its throat with a sharp blade. I feel this is similar to our situation. I've been stalking you for so long that you've tired. And now you are laying down, asking for death. But I fear for you that it won't come quickly," Patrick said, taking out a black and white composition notebook and setting it gently on the table.

"This is for Special Agent Adams. He'll find it when he finds you, which might not be for a while. Oh, and this light is on a battery. I could wager to say it might last a few days, but after that, you'll be in total darkness."

"But, I thought you were going to kill me quickly?"

"I lied, Dr. Benson. I thought about how to torture and prolong your death. With you, I needed it to be a reflection of the time I put in. So, you will stay here, and you will starve to death, Dr. Benson. It will be the most unpleasant torture you can imagine. It will give you ample time sit in the dark and reflect on your life and face your death. You will review your time on Earth and what you have done with it. I imagine it will be quite glorious, Dr. Benson."

"No, Patrick, please, just kill me. Please. "

"There was a time when you begged me to let you live, now you beg for me to kill you. I'm proud of you, Dr. Benson, you've grown. Goodbye, Dr. Benson. I will cherish our time together."

"Patrick!" Dr. Benson sobbed. "Please don't do this!"

Patrick started to walk out the door and head on his way when Dr. Benson shouted, "Wait!"

Patrick turned around.

"Why me, Patrick? Why did you pick me? Of all people."

"Because Dr. Benson. You have been judged, and found wanting." Patrick closed the door and locked the padlock, sealing them alone in their tomb.

"NO!" Dr. Benson screamed at the top of his lungs.

★★★★★★★★★★

Patrick turned the key to Dr. Benson's car, and the engine roared to life. The sun was starting to set, and the open road lay ahead of him. With a full tank of gas, he looked toward the passenger seat.

"Are you ready, Arthur?" Patrick asked.

"I've always wanted to see the Pacific Ocean," Arthur replied.

★★★★★★★★★★

Tiny amounts of water trickled down cracks in the concrete of the bunker, finally making their way to the floor. It had been seventeen days since Dr. Benson had anything that could be called a meal. Mayor Jenkins had been dead for nearly two weeks, leaving Dr. Benson alone with his thoughts. The tomb that contained Dr. Benson smelled of feces from both men. Sores engulfed Dr. Benson's loose and pale skin. Some cracked open and began to secrete puss and blood. His breathing was labored, and if his shirt was off, you could see every single one of his ribs struggle to lift.

"Tommy!" Dr. Benson yelled to no one in the blackness. His body was eating his brain, and he had been hallucinating about the only thing on his mind.

"I'm sorry! Don't run! I just want to say I'm sorry!"

With his head hung down, he swung his arm to his left to feel the water jugs all lying on their sides, completely empty. With barely the energy to talk, he faintly had a thought about wishing he had used the single bullet on himself.

"Jenkins! Tommy! Get back here!"

From having hopes of being a world-renowned doctor and writing books to being chained up in the makeshift dungeon of a crazy, Dr. Benson's body took its last breath. His shoulders slumped down just a bit further and never moved again. There he sat, The Great Dr. Benson, dumbfounded as to how a man named Arthur Fritz got the best of him. He spent his final days in the dark, contemplating his life and thinking of Tommy B., Cornelius, Mayor Jenkins, and of course Patrick.

THIRTY-TWO

"Total paranoia is just total awareness."

-Charles Manson; Manson Family Cult Leader; Cincinnati Ohio, USA

S pecial Agent Adams caught his eureka moment in the county assessor's office six weeks after the disappearance of Mayor Jenkins and Dr. Benson. He had spent weeks searching for deeds and titles to everything under the names Arthur Fritz and Patrick Leopold. After digging through nearly every record in every office of New Hope, he found a small patch of land, deeded from an Arthur Fritz to a George Felter.

"Why does that name sound familiar? I remember reading that name somewhere."

As he ran out of the assessor's office and into his car, he flipped through his notebook where every detail that he found had been captured. After flipping back and forth, he finally found it.

"George Felter! Arthur's friend at the hospital. That mean old bastard who wants to fight everyone! Son of a bitch."

Special Agent Adams followed a barely visible road into a patch of trees until he came to a clearing and the road ended. Adams double checked his map and ensured he was in the right spot. After scanning around, a reflection of light from something caught his eye just on the other side of the clearing.

"Aha!"

With a jolt of gusto, he ran across the meadow, treading through patches of snow and wet spots, soaking and muddying his pants. Breathing heavily, he reached a bunker that looked exactly like the other one. He walked around until he found the stairs on the opposite side.

"Is anyone in there?" he yelled.

There was no reply. After two gunshots, the lock finally broke off and fell to the ground. He knew what he would find in there, he just had to confirm. He kicked open the door to find the grizzly scene inside. A shrunken Dr. Benson and a hunched over Mayor Jenkins, well preserved from the cold. He looked over on the table to find a notebook with a note on the cover addressed to Special Agent Adams.

Special Agent Adams,

I hope this note finds you well, and I hope for your sake it finds you before summer. Enjoy these memoirs as I took great pride in writing them down. They are a peek inside my mind and some of my general thoughts. I think you will enjoy them. They might give you a clue of where and how to find me. I look forward to meeting you one day.

-Patrick

Special Agent Adams just shook his head. He realized that Arthur had left Dr. Benson to starve to death. Next to him were three empty water jugs.

"That sick fuck. He must have left water for him, knowing he would die slower with only water and no food."

Back outside, Agent Adams rhythmically tapped the rolled-up composition notebook against his leg, squinting from the sun, but also from how close he was to stopping the two deaths. If he had only found the connection sooner, he thought inside his head. Adams took a seat in the sun, leaning up against the log roof of the bunker. The grass high up on his ankles, he took a cigarette out from his jacket pocket and lit it up. Letting out a big puff of smoke, he began to read the memoirs.

★★★★★★★★★★

Special Agent Adams had stopped at the first pay phone he found on the way back into New Hope. After calling Chief Nelson and giving him the news on Mayor Jenkins and Dr. Benson, he made a call to Washington.

"Senator Young? It's Adams."

"Well, what's the word?" the senator replied.

"I'm headed West. I want to head up a task force for a nationwide manhunt for Arthur Fritz."

The following is a sneak peek of the much-
anticipated sequel to Memoirs of a Crazy:

CONFESSIONS OF A CRAZY

The landscape blurred past as Dr. Benson's Chevelle
flew down the two-lane road laden with cracks in
the asphalt. With the sun in his eyes, Patrick had a
broad smile across his stubble-rich face. With his
right hand loosely on the wheel and his left hanging
on the window ledge, he turned to look at Arthur
sitting in the passenger seat.

"Are you okay, Arthur?"

Arthur sat, stoic and silent, mostly reflecting on the
past events and a little bit on the future.

"I'll say to you, good sir, I feel great. That
was an adventure," Patrick said, trying to keep the
dialogue flowing. "I wonder what Dr. Benson is
thinking about right now?"

"I imagine he's quite upset."

"What about you Arthur? Are you upset?"

"I'm just fine, Patrick. I have been thinking
of your last line to Harold. You've been judged and
found wanting. Why that? What does it mean?
That's something God would say."

"Why you're exactly right, Arthur. That is something God would say. And, I'll let you in on a little secret."

"Oh, yeah? What's that?"

"I am God."

Thank you for purchasing and reading Memoirs of a Crazy. I hope you enjoyed reading it as much as I enjoyed writing it. Please leave me a review on Amazon so that others can share your experience.

I love connecting with readers. Feel free to connect with me on the following:

www.facebook.com/charlesmbooks
www.charlesmbooks.com
@charlesmbooks

Thank you!

Charles M.